Also by Rachael Reed

Sis
Sis 2 Blood on the Streets

Standalone
Codefendant
Codefendant
Once a Cheater
Once a Cheater
Passport Bro
What Happens in Prison
Preference
Sprinkle Sprinkle
Championship Bad
Street Exodus
Street Exodus
Street Royalty
Pawns of Power
SIS
Cartel Bloodline
Get Money Girls
Skip the Games
Til Death Do Us Part

Backpage Hustle
Link in Bio
The Virgin and The Kingpin
A Gangsta's Heart
Boosters
Can't Turn a Hoe Into a Housewife

Sis
2
Blood on the Streets

Rachael Reed

Check Out More Great Products and Free Giveaways
https://tbdbpublishing.com/

Chapter 1: The Funeral

The stale, suffocating air of the funeral home clung to Jasmine's skin like a second layer of sweat. Her mother, Miss Loretta, laid out in a coffin, didn't look nothing like the strong woman Jasmine remembered. The mortician tried to cover up the bullet wounds with makeup, but Jasmine could still see the deep, jagged scars beneath. It was like a cruel joke, dressing up a body that had been torn apart by the streets. The streets that had taken everything from her.

Jasmine stood stiff, her fists clenched at her sides, struggling to keep it together. Her heart ached with a pain so deep it was like someone had reached inside her chest and ripped it out. She wanted to scream, to cry, but all she could do was stand there, staring down at her mother's lifeless face.

The room was filled with people, but Jasmine couldn't hear nothing over the roar in her head. The whispers, the looks—she knew they was talking about her, about how the Black Knights had sent a message by taking out Miss Loretta. They were waiting to see if Jasmine would break, but she wasn't about to give them that satisfaction.

Tasha, her ride-or-die since they was kids, sidled up beside her, her voice barely a whisper. "Jas, you good?" Tasha's words were cautious, like she was scared Jasmine might snap any second.

"Good? Nah, I ain't good, Tash," Jasmine muttered, her voice thick with grief. "I'mma make sure them niggas pay for what they did to Ma. They ain't just took her from me, they declared war."

Tasha glanced around the room, her eyes nervous, but Jasmine didn't care who heard. Let them run and tell it—let the Black Knights know she was coming for them. The time for playing nice was long gone.

As they headed to the gravesite, Jasmine stepped outside, the hot Virginia sun beating down on her like it had a personal vendetta. The streets were alive with whispers, the kind that made the hairs on the back of your neck stand up. Word traveled fast in the hood, and everybody knew by now that Miss Loretta had been gunned down in cold blood. The Black Knights had made their move, and now it was Jasmine's turn.

As she walked down the cracked sidewalk, heads turned, and conversations hushed. The respect was there, but it was laced with fear—fear of what Jasmine might do next. And she wanted them to be scared, because she was scared too. Scared of the anger that was boiling inside her, scared of what she might become now that she had nothing left to lose.

A group of corner boys who had known Ms, Loretta since they were babies watched her with wide eyes as she passed by. One of them, a skinny kid with too-big clothes, muttered something to his friend, and they both looked away quickly when Jasmine's icy stare landed on them. They knew better than to mess with her right now. Hell, everybody kept their distance, sensing the danger rolling off her in waves.

Jasmine's mind was a whirlwind, her thoughts racing a mile a minute. She needed to get her head straight, to figure out how she was gonna hit back. The Black Knights had made this personal, and Jasmine wasn't about to let them walk away unscathed. She was gonna make them bleed, just like they made her mother bleed.

The cemetery was eerily quiet, the only sound the rustle of dry leaves in the wind. Jasmine stood at the edge of the grave, her heart heavy as she watched them lower her mother into the ground. It felt final, like she was losing her all over again. The weight of it threatened to crush her, but she couldn't let herself break down. Not here, not now.

She knelt down, grabbing a handful of dirt and letting it slip through her fingers. "I'mma make this right, Ma. I swear on everything, I ain't lettin' them get away with this," she whispered, her voice cracking with emotion. The tears that she'd held back all day finally spilled over, hot and bitter. She didn't wipe them away.

The priest droned on in the background, talking 'bout peace and forgiveness, but Jasmine wasn't trying to hear none of that. There was no peace in her heart, no room for forgiveness. Only a burning need for revenge. The kind of revenge that would send a message to the entire damn city: Jasmine was not to be fucked with.

The walk back from the cemetery was long, the air thick with tension. Jasmine could feel it in the way people looked at her, the way they whispered when they thought she couldn't hear. The Black Knights had crossed a line, and the whole hood was waiting to see what Jasmine would do about it.

She stopped at the corner store, the dingy little place where her mother used to send her for milk when she was just a kid. The memories stabbed at her, sharp and painful, but she pushed them down. She had work to do.

The store was packed with people, all of them pretending not to notice Jasmine as she walked in. The clerk behind the counter, an old man who'd known Miss Loretta for years, gave her a look that was equal parts pity and fear. He knew what was up. They all did.

Jasmine grabbed a bottle of Henny, the glass cool and solid in her hand, and slapped it on the counter. "Put it on my tab," she said, her voice cold and hard as steel. The clerk nodded quickly, not daring to argue.

As she turned to leave, she spotted a familiar face lurking in the back of the store. Chris, one of the Black Knights' enforcers, was watching her with a mix of curiosity and caution. He was a small-time thug, nothing special, but he was connected, and right now, Jasmine needed information.

She walked over to him, her steps slow and deliberate. Chris shifted nervously, glancing around like he was looking for an exit. "Chris," Jasmine said, her voice low and dangerous. "You got somethin' to say?"

Chris swallowed hard, his eyes darting around the store. "Jas, I ain't got nothin' to do with what happened to your moms. I swear," he stammered, his voice shaky.

"I know you didn't," Jasmine replied, her tone icy. "But you know who did. And you gonna tell me, or I'mma make sure you regret it."

Chris's eyes widened in fear, and he quickly nodded. "Aight, aight. It was Killa Kev. They the ones who pulled the trigger. Word is, he was sendin' a message."

Jasmine's blood ran cold, her fists clenching at her sides. Killa Kev was one of the Black Knights' top hitters, a ruthless killer who didn't give a damn about nothing but money and power. And now he was the target of Jasmine's wrath.

"Where he at?" Jasmine demanded, her voice a low growl.

"Last I heard, he was layin' low at his girl's place over on 5th Street," Chris answered quickly, eager to be rid of her.

Jasmine nodded, satisfied. "You ain't seen me, Chris. Remember that."

Without waiting for a response, Jasmine turned and walked out of the store, her mind already working out a plan. Killa Kev was gonna pay, and he was gonna pay in blood.

The sun had set by the time Jasmine made her way to 5th Street. The block was quiet, too quiet, and that made Jasmine's nerves tingle. She moved through the shadows like a ghost, her steps silent as she approached the run-down apartment building where Killa Kev's girl lived.

Jasmine had been around the block enough times to know how this game worked. Killa Kev wasn't stupid—he'd have lookouts posted, and he'd be ready for trouble. But Jasmine had the element of surprise, and she was gonna use it.

She slipped around to the back of the building, her heart pounding in her chest. The fire escape was rusted and creaky, but Jasmine climbed it with ease, keeping her movements slow and deliberate. When she reached the third floor, she peered into the window, her eyes narrowing as she spotted Killa Kev inside, sitting on the couch with a blunt in one hand and his phone in the other.

Jasmine's grip tightened on the piece tucked into her waistband. She took a deep breath, steadying herself, then slid the window open, slipping inside like a shadow. Killa Kev didn't even hear her coming until it was too late.

"Kev," Jasmine said, her voice cold and steady. He turned, his eyes widening in shock as he saw her standing there, gun in hand.

"Jas—" he started, but she didn't let him finish. The shot rang out, deafening in the small room, and Killa Kev crumpled to the floor, blood pooling around him. Jasmine stared down at him, her breath coming in ragged gasps.

It was done. But instead of feeling satisfied, Jasmine felt empty. The revenge she'd craved didn't bring her the closure she'd hoped for. The anger was still there, burning hotter than ever.

She turned and left the apartment, her mind already racing with what came next. Killa Kev was just the beginning. The Black Knights had declared war, and Jasmine was gonna finish it

Chapter 2: The Call to Arms

The night was thick with the scent of rain and gunpowder as Jasmine made her way to the abandoned warehouse on the edge of town. It was their spot, a place where plans were made and blood oaths were sworn. The wind whipped through the broken windows, carrying the echoes of the city's darkest corners. Jasmine's mind was racing, every step she took echoing her resolve. The war had begun, and she needed to pull her people together.

Inside the warehouse, the dim light from a flickering bulb cast long shadows on the cracked concrete floors. Her crew was already there, a collection of hustlers, street soldiers, and hitters who had been with her through thick and thin. They were waiting for her, their eyes filled with a mix of respect and anticipation. Jasmine didn't keep them waiting.

She walked into the center of the room, her presence commanding. The conversations stopped, and all eyes were on her. Marcus, her right-hand man, stood off to the side, his face as unreadable as ever. He was a big dude, the kind that didn't need to say much to get his point across. He and Jasmine had been through hell together, and she knew she could trust him with her life.

"Alright, y'all," Jasmine began, her voice low but carrying weight. "Y'all know what went down. Black Knights crossed a line they can't come back from. They took my moms, and now we taking everything they got."

A murmur of agreement rippled through the crew, but Jasmine raised a hand to silence them. "I ain't just talking 'bout a couple of drive-bys or some weak-ass retaliation. We goin' for the jugular. We ain't just takin' out their soldiers—we takin' out their money, their connections, their whole damn empire."

Marcus stepped forward, his voice deep and steady. "Jas, we with you. But we gotta be smart 'bout this. We can't just go in guns blazing. We gotta hit 'em where it hurts, make sure they don't get back up."

Jasmine nodded, her eyes locked on Marcus. "Exactly. That's why I need all y'all to be ready for what's coming. This ain't just business—this is personal. And I don't plan on losin.'"

After the meeting, Jasmine pulled Marcus aside. They needed more than just their core crew to take down the Black Knights. They needed muscle, firepower, and connections that stretched beyond their usual reach. Jasmine had a plan, but it required getting some new blood involved.

"Marcus, I need you to reach out to some folks," Jasmine said, her voice low and urgent. "We need to bring in the Southside Kings. I know they got beef with the Knights too, and they'll be down to ride if the price is right."

Marcus raised an eyebrow, considering. "The Southside Kings ain't exactly known for playin' nice, Jas. They ruthless, even by our standards."

"I know that," Jasmine shot back. "But we need that kinda energy. We gotta send a message that we ain't just fightin' for territory—we fightin' for survival."

Marcus nodded slowly, his mind already working through the logistics. "Aight. I'll set up a meet. But you know if we bring them in, we gotta be ready for shit to get real messy."

Jasmine's eyes were cold, her resolve unshakable. "Let it get messy. I'm done playin' by their rules. It's time to rewrite the game."

The next few days were a blur of activity. Jasmine moved like a woman possessed, hitting up every contact she had, calling in favors, and stacking up resources. She secured a fresh shipment of guns, courtesy of a smuggler who owed her a favor, and got her hands on some heavy artillery that would give them an edge.

Jasmine also reached out to an old flame, Cal, who had connections in the underground fight scene. He was a rough dude, all muscle and scars, but he had a crew of fighters who could double as enforcers when the time came. They were exactly the kind of backup Jasmine needed.

She met Cal in a grimy bar on the outskirts of town, a place where the drinks were cheap and the cops stayed away. Cal was leaning against the bar, his eyes lighting up when he saw her.

"Jas, long time no see," Cal drawled, his voice dripping with that dangerous charm that had drawn her in years ago. "Heard you been busy."

"Busy don't even begin to cover it," Jasmine replied, sliding onto the stool beside him. "I need your help, Cal. Shit's about to go down, and I need muscle—your kind of muscle."

Cal smirked, taking a swig of his drink. "You know my boys don't come cheap."

Jasmine leaned in, her eyes locking onto his. "This ain't about money, Cal. This is about respect. You help me take down the Black Knights, and you'll have the streets eatin' outta your hand. That's worth more than cash."

Cal considered her words, then nodded slowly. "Aight, Jas. I'm in. But when this is over, you and me? We gotta settle some unfinished business."

Jasmine didn't flinch. "We'll see, Cal. We'll see."

With the pieces in place, Jasmine called another meeting, this time with the expanded crew. The warehouse was more crowded now, filled with new faces—Southside Kings, Cal's fighters, and other street soldiers who had been drawn in by the promise of taking down the Black Knights.

Jasmine stood before them, her presence commanding the room. She laid out the plan in detail, every move calculated, every angle covered. There was no room for mistakes, no second chances.

"We hittin' 'em hard and fast," Jasmine said, her voice strong, cutting through the tension. "First, we take out their suppliers. Without their product, they ain't got no cash flow. Then we go for their stash houses, their safe spots. We gonna make it so they got nowhere to run, nowhere to hide."

Marcus stepped up beside her, his voice steady and calm. "Y'all know the risks. This ain't a game. We goin' up against killers. But we got the upper hand, 'cause we got the element of surprise. We keep that on our side, and we'll come out on top."

The room buzzed with anticipation, the air thick with the promise of violence. Jasmine looked around, meeting the eyes of every person there, making sure they understood what was at stake.

"This ain't just about revenge," Jasmine continued, her voice dropping to a dangerous whisper. "This is about takin' back what's ours. The Black Knights think they can run these streets, but they forgot one thing—they forgot who they messin' with."

The crew erupted into a low murmur of agreement, their resolve hardening. They were ready. The plan was set, and the clock was ticking. Jasmine felt a cold satisfaction settle in her chest. This was it. The beginning of the end for the Black Knights.

As the meeting broke up, Marcus pulled Jasmine aside, his face serious. "Jas, you sure 'bout this? We all in now. Ain't no turning back."

Jasmine looked him dead in the eye, her voice unwavering. "I'm sure, Marcus. This is what we gotta do. For Ma. For everything they took from us."

Marcus nodded, his expression grim. "Aight, then. Let's finish this."

Jasmine watched as the crew filed out of the warehouse, her heart pounding with a mix of fear and anticipation. The war had begun, and there was no going back now. The streets were about to run red, and Jasmine was ready to see it through to the bitter end.

As she stood there, alone in the empty warehouse, a sense of finality settled over her. The next move was hers, and she was gonna make damn sure it was a move the Black Knights would never forget.

Chapter 3: Striking Back

The night was thick with tension, the kind that made your skin crawl and your senses go on high alert. Jasmine stood in the shadows outside one of the Black Knights' stash houses, a rundown trap on the east side that looked as dead as the junkies that haunted its corners. She could feel the weight of the piece tucked in her waistband, the cold metal pressing against her skin, a reminder of what was about to go down.

Her crew was in position, spread out around the block like wolves closing in on their prey. Jasmine had planned every detail of this hit down to the last second. She wasn't just looking to send a message—she was looking to cripple the Black Knights, to tear their empire down brick by brick.

"Y'all ready?" Jasmine whispered into the comms, her voice low and steady.

"Ready, Jas," Marcus's voice crackled back. He was posted up by the back door, his Glock at the ready, his eyes scanning the darkness for any signs of movement.

"Good. On my count," Jasmine instructed, her pulse quickening. She glanced over at Tasha, who was crouched beside her, her face a mask of determination. This was it—the moment they'd been building up to.

Jasmine counted down from three, her voice barely a breath, and then all hell broke loose.

They hit the stash house hard and fast, busting through the doors with a fury that took the Black Knights completely by surprise. The sound of gunfire erupted in the small space, bullets tearing through the air, ripping into bodies, and shattering the silence of the night. Jasmine moved with a lethal grace, her gun steady in her hand as she took down anyone who got in her way.

The Black Knights fought back, but they were disorganized, caught off guard by the ferocity of Jasmine's crew. Jasmine could see the fear in their eyes, the realization that they weren't dealing with just another rival crew—they were dealing with someone who had nothing left to lose.

Within minutes, the stash house was a war zone, bodies slumped against the walls, blood pooling on the floor. Jasmine stood in the middle of the carnage, her chest heaving with adrenaline, her eyes cold and hard as steel. She wasn't done yet—not by a long shot.

"Burn it," Jasmine ordered, her voice devoid of emotion. Tasha nodded, already setting the place up with gasoline-soaked rags and a lighter. In seconds, the flames roared to life, consuming everything in their path.

As they walked away, the fire lit up the night sky, a beacon of the war that had just begun.

Word spread through the streets like wildfire—Jasmine had struck back, and she'd struck hard. The Black Knights were reeling from the loss, their operations crippled, their soldiers dead or running scared. But Jasmine knew better than to think they'd just lie down and take it. She'd been in this game long enough to know that every action had a reaction, and she was ready for it.

But the retaliation came faster and harder than she'd expected.

It was a couple of nights later when the Black Knights made their move. Jasmine and her crew were posted up at one of their own spots, a small house on the west side where they stored their weapons and cash. They were laying low, waiting for the heat to die down, but the Black Knights weren't giving them that luxury.

Jasmine was in the middle of a conversation with Marcus when the first shots rang out. The windows shattered, glass spraying across the room as bullets tore through the walls. Jasmine hit the floor, her heart racing as she reached for her gun. The air was thick with smoke and the acrid smell of gunpowder, the sound of gunfire deafening in the small space.

"They found us!" Tasha yelled, scrambling for cover behind an overturned table.

"Stay down! Return fire!" Jasmine shouted, her voice cutting through the chaos. She fired back, the recoil of the gun sending shocks up her arm as she tried to keep her breathing steady.

The Black Knights weren't holding back—they'd come with a vengeance, determined to wipe Jasmine and her crew off the map. The firefight raged on, the sound of bullets ricocheting off walls and tearing through flesh filling the air.

Jasmine's mind was racing, calculating her next move. They couldn't stay here—this place was compromised, and the Black Knights were coming in strong. She needed to get her crew out of there before they were all dead.

"Marcus, we gotta fall back! We can't hold this spot!" Jasmine shouted over the noise.

Marcus nodded, his face grim as he fired off a few more shots. "Aight, we out! Everyone move, now!"

They scrambled for the back door, ducking and weaving as bullets whizzed past them. Jasmine could feel the adrenaline pumping through her veins, her senses on high alert as she led the way out. The night air hit her like a slap in the face, cold and sharp, but there was no time to catch her breath.

The Black Knights were right on their heels, and Jasmine knew they had to keep moving if they wanted to survive the night.

Jasmine and her crew tore through the alleyways, their footsteps echoing off the brick walls as they ran. The city was a maze of darkness and danger, every corner a potential ambush, every shadow a hiding place for death. Jasmine's heart was pounding in her chest, her breath coming in short, ragged gasps as she pushed herself to keep going.

They needed a safe spot, somewhere they could regroup and plan their next move. But right now, safety felt like a distant dream.

"Jas, where we headed?" Tasha asked, her voice strained as she struggled to keep up.

"Safehouse on 14th," Jasmine replied, her mind racing as she tried to plot the quickest route. "We lay low there, figure out our next move."

Marcus was bringing up the rear, his eyes scanning their surroundings for any sign of the Black Knights. "They ain't gonna stop, Jas. They out for blood now."

"I know," Jasmine said, her voice cold. "But so am I."

They reached the safehouse, a run-down apartment in a forgotten part of the city, and Jasmine wasted no time getting them inside. The place was a dump, but it had solid walls and a few good locks on the doors, and right now, that was all that mattered.

Once inside, Jasmine collapsed onto a worn-out couch, her mind still racing. The Black Knights had hit back hard, but she wasn't about to let them think they'd won. This was just the beginning, and Jasmine was ready to take this fight all the way.

But the exhaustion was creeping in, the adrenaline wearing off and leaving her feeling drained and raw. She knew she couldn't afford to rest—not with the Black Knights out there, hunting her down. But for a moment, just a moment, she let herself close her eyes and breathe.

"Jas," Marcus's voice broke through the haze of exhaustion, pulling her back to reality. "We gotta be smart 'bout this. They ain't just gonna come at us—they gonna come at everyone we care about."

Jasmine's eyes snapped open, her heart skipping a beat at the thought. Her mind flashed to the people she'd tried to keep out of this mess—her little brother, her few remaining friends who weren't in the game. The Black Knights would go after them, use them as leverage, and that thought made her blood run cold.

"We can't let that happen," Jasmine said, her voice steely with resolve. "We hit them first. Harder than ever. We take away everything they got before they even think about touching what's mine."

Jasmine's resolve hardened as she sat up, the fatigue pushed aside by the urgency of the situation. There was no time to waste—she needed to hit the Black Knights before they had a chance to regroup or retaliate. Jasmine motioned for Tasha and Marcus to gather around, pulling a battered map of the city from her bag and spreading it out on the coffee table.

"We need to move fast," Jasmine said, her voice sharp with determination. "They think they can back us into a corner, but we're about to flip this on 'em. We ain't just playin' defense no more—we're takin' the fight to them."

Tasha leaned in, her eyes narrowing as she studied the map. "So, what's the plan, Jas? Where we hittin' next?"

Jasmine pointed to a cluster of red circles she'd marked on the map, locations she knew were crucial to the Black Knights' operations. "We're goin' after their supply chain. Without that, they're nothing. We hit their distribution centers, their stash spots, and their transport routes. We're gonna choke off their cash flow until they're beggin' for air."

Marcus nodded, his expression grim. "That's gonna hurt 'em, no doubt. But it's gonna take more than just us to pull this off."

"I know," Jasmine replied, her mind already calculating their next move. "That's why we're bringing in some extra muscle. I got Cal's crew on standby, and the Southside Kings are ready to ride. We hit 'em with everything we got, all at once. They won't know what hit 'em."

Tasha smirked, a glint of excitement in her eyes. "You really think we can pull this off?"

Jasmine met her gaze, her expression deadly serious. "We ain't got a choice, Tash. It's do or die."

The room fell silent as the weight of Jasmine's words settled over them. They all knew the stakes—this wasn't just about taking down the Black Knights anymore. It was about survival, about protecting everything they held dear. Jasmine could see the determination in their faces, the same fire that was burning in her own chest.

"Alright, then," Marcus said, breaking the silence. "Let's get to work."

The night air was thick with tension as Jasmine and her crew moved through the darkened streets. The city was eerily quiet, the kind of silence that only came before a storm. Jasmine's heart was pounding in her chest, her senses on high alert as they approached their first target—a warehouse on the outskirts of town, one of the Black Knights' main distribution hubs.

Jasmine signaled for her crew to fan out, each of them taking up positions around the building. She could feel the adrenaline coursing through her veins, her mind sharp and focused. This was it—the moment of truth. She wasn't just out for revenge anymore. She was out to destroy everything the Black Knights had built.

"On my mark," Jasmine whispered into the comms, her eyes locked on the warehouse entrance. "Three... two... one... go!"

The crew moved in with lethal precision, bursting through the doors and taking down the guards before they even had a chance to react. The warehouse erupted into chaos as Jasmine's crew tore through the building, taking out anyone who dared to stand in their way.

Jasmine moved through the chaos with a cold efficiency, her gun steady in her hand as she cleared room after room. The Black Knights were scrambling, their operations falling apart under the weight of the assault. Jasmine could see the fear in their eyes, the realization that they were up against something far more dangerous than they'd ever anticipated.

"Clear!" Marcus's voice rang out over the comms as the last of the resistance was crushed. The warehouse was theirs, and with it, a major blow had been dealt to the Black Knights.

But Jasmine knew this was just the beginning.

"Burn it," she ordered, her voice ice-cold. Tasha and a couple of others immediately got to work, setting the place up to go up in flames. Jasmine watched as the fire consumed everything, the heat licking at her skin, the flames reflecting in her eyes.

She didn't flinch.

The victory was short-lived. The Black Knights weren't about to roll over and die. Just hours after Jasmine's crew took down the warehouse, word came in that the Black Knights had struck back, and they'd done it with brutal efficiency.

Jasmine's phone buzzed with a message from one of her informants—a photo of one of their safe houses, now a smoking ruin, bodies strewn across the yard. The Black Knights had retaliated hard, and they weren't playing games.

Jasmine's stomach turned as she stared at the image, the reality of the situation crashing down on her. This wasn't just a war—it was a blood feud, and it was spiraling out of control.

"They hit back," Marcus said, his voice grim as he looked over her shoulder at the photo. "They ain't gonna stop, Jas. This shit's getting real messy."

Jasmine's jaw tightened, her resolve hardening. "Then we keep hitting 'em. We don't stop 'til they're wiped out."

Tasha nodded, but there was a flicker of doubt in her eyes. "Jas... we gotta think this through. We ain't just fighting for territory anymore. We're fighting for our lives."

Jasmine knew she was right, but she couldn't back down now. Not after everything they'd lost, everything they'd fought for. The Black Knights had to be stopped, no matter the cost.

"We're too deep in this to back out," Jasmine said, her voice steady. "We hit them harder, faster. We take out their leadership, cripple them from the top down. This ain't gonna end until one of us is left standing."

Marcus and Tasha exchanged a look, then nodded. They were all in, just like Jasmine.

But as they prepared for the next strike, a sense of unease settled over Jasmine, a gnawing feeling in the pit of her stomach. The violence was escalating, spinning out of control, and she knew that the line between victory and defeat was razor-thin.

But there was no turning back now.

As Jasmine and her crew prepared for the next round of attacks, she received an unexpected call. The voice on the other end was calm, measured, and chillingly familiar.

"Jasmine," the voice said, sending a shiver down her spine. "You're making a lot of noise. But you should know, the Black Knights ain't the only ones watching."

Jasmine's heart skipped a beat. She recognized the voice—it belonged to an old rival, someone she hadn't crossed paths with in years. Someone who had the power to tip the scales in this war.

"What do you want?" Jasmine demanded, her voice steady despite the fear creeping up her spine.

"Just a friendly warning," the voice replied, a hint of amusement in the tone. "You keep pushing, and you're gonna find yourself in a fight you can't win. The streets don't belong to you, Jasmine. And there are bigger players out there who don't take kindly to you stirring up trouble."

The line went dead, leaving Jasmine standing in the middle of the safehouse, the phone still clutched in her hand. A cold dread settled over her, the realization that the war she'd started was about to get a whole lot bigger—and a whole lot deadlier.

She had thought the Black Knights were the biggest threat she'd face, but now she knew better. The streets were a jungle, and there were predators lurking in the shadows, waiting to strike.

As she lowered the phone, her resolve only grew stronger. The stakes had just been raised, but Jasmine wasn't backing down. Not now, not ever.

This was her war, and she was gonna see it through to the bitter end—no matter who came after her next.

Chapter 4: The Empire in Crisis

The safehouse was quieter than usual, a tension hanging in the air so thick you could cut it with a knife. Jasmine stood at the window, staring out into the dark streets, her mind racing with the weight of the decisions she had to make. The war with the Black Knights had taken its toll on her crew—people were getting paranoid, loyalty was wavering, and the cracks were starting to show.

Behind her, Tasha and Marcus were deep in conversation, their voices low and serious. Jasmine could feel the unease creeping up on her, a gnawing fear that something was about to go very wrong. She knew the streets were watching, waiting for any sign of weakness, and right now, her empire was teetering on the edge.

"Jas, we gotta talk," Marcus said, breaking her out of her thoughts. He sounded troubled, more so than usual, and that alone set off alarm bells in Jasmine's head.

"Yeah, what's up?" Jasmine asked, turning to face him. She could see the worry etched on his face, and that sent a chill down her spine.

"There's been talk," Marcus said slowly, choosing his words carefully. "People sayin' there's a rat in the crew. Some of the moves we made, the Black Knights was ready for 'em. It ain't just bad luck."

Jasmine's heart skipped a beat. A rat. The word echoed in her mind like a death sentence. She knew what it meant—a traitor, someone who was feeding the enemy information. Someone who could bring her entire operation crashing down.

"Who's talking?" Jasmine demanded, her voice hard. She couldn't afford to show any sign of weakness, not now. Not when everything was hanging by a thread.

"Word is, it's Big Moe," Tasha cut in, her tone grim. "He been actin' real shady lately, disappearin' at odd hours, makin' calls he ain't supposed to. And then there's Tiny... he got ties to folks who might not be on our side."

Jasmine clenched her fists, her mind racing. Big Moe was one of her top earners, someone she'd trusted with a lot of responsibility. But if he was the rat... she couldn't let that slide.

"Get him in here," Jasmine ordered, her voice cold as ice. "And bring Tiny too. We gonna get to the bottom of this."

The tension in the room was suffocating as Big Moe and Tiny were brought in, both of them looking uneasy as they stood before Jasmine. She sat behind the table, her eyes narrowing as she studied them, trying to read their faces, their body language. They looked nervous, but she couldn't tell if it was guilt or just fear of the situation they were in.

"Y'all know why you here," Jasmine began, her voice low and deadly. "I've been hearin' some shit, and I ain't liking it. Somebody in this crew been playin' both sides, and I need to know who it is."

Big Moe shifted on his feet, his eyes darting around the room. "Jas, I ain't no snitch. You know me. I been down with you since day one."

"That's what you say," Jasmine shot back, her gaze never leaving his face. "But I got folks tellin' me you been actin' shady, makin' moves behind my back. You wanna explain that?"

Big Moe's face twisted into a look of desperation. "Jas, I swear, it ain't like that. I been out there hustlin', tryin' to keep the money flowin'. You know how it is—sometimes you gotta do what you gotta do."

Jasmine's eyes flicked over to Tiny, who had been uncharacteristically quiet. "And you, Tiny? You been movin' funny too. What you gotta say for yourself?"

Tiny finally looked up, meeting Jasmine's gaze with a steady, unreadable expression. "I'm loyal, Jas. You know that. But you gotta be careful who you trust out here. Not everyone got your back like they say they do."

Jasmine felt a knot tighten in her stomach. She needed to make a decision, and she needed to make it fast. The longer this dragged on, the more damage it would do to her crew, to her empire. She couldn't afford to let the doubt fester.

"Loyalty ain't just words, Tiny," Jasmine said, her voice sharp. "It's actions. And right now, I need to know if y'all are with me or against me."

There was a long, heavy silence as the words hung in the air. Big Moe and Tiny exchanged a quick glance, something unspoken passing between them that made Jasmine's heart sink. She knew then—there was no coming back from this.

"Marcus," Jasmine said, her voice barely above a whisper. "You know what to do."

Marcus nodded, his expression hardening as he stepped forward. "Aight, Jas."

Before either of them could react, Marcus pulled out his gun, aiming it squarely at Big Moe. The sound of the shot echoed through the room, deafening in the silence that followed. Big Moe crumpled to the floor, a pool of blood spreading out beneath him.

Jasmine's heart pounded in her chest as she watched him fall, the reality of what she'd just done crashing over her like a wave. But there was no time for regret, no time for second thoughts. This was the life she'd chosen, and she had to see it through.

Tiny didn't flinch, his expression remaining cold and impassive. "You made your point, Jas," he said quietly. "But you gotta be careful. This shit's gonna come back on you."

Jasmine met his gaze, her eyes hard. "I ain't scared, Tiny. This is my empire, and I'mma do whatever it takes to keep it."

The air in the safehouse was thick with tension as the crew processed what had just happened. Big Moe had been one of their own, and now he was gone, taken out by Jasmine's order. The message was clear—disloyalty wouldn't be tolerated. But it came at a cost.

Jasmine could feel the eyes of her crew on her, the doubt creeping in. She knew some of them were questioning her decisions, wondering if she'd gone too far. But she couldn't let that show. She had to stay strong, to keep control of the situation before it spiraled out of her hands.

"We can't afford no weak links," Jasmine said, her voice cutting through the silence. "This war ain't just 'bout takin' out the Black Knights. It's 'bout survival. If you ain't with me 100%, then you best walk away now, 'cause I ain't gonna hesitate to do what needs to be done."

There was a murmur of agreement, but Jasmine could see the unease in their faces. The line had been drawn, and they all knew it. There was no turning back.

Marcus approached her as the crew began to disperse, his expression unreadable. "You did what you had to do, Jas," he said quietly. "But we gotta be careful. Shit's getting out of hand."

Jasmine nodded, exhaustion creeping into her bones. "I know, Marcus. But we ain't got no choice. We either keep pushin' forward, or we get buried."

Marcus sighed, running a hand over his face. "Yeah, but how many more we gonna lose before this is over?"

Jasmine didn't have an answer. All she knew was that she couldn't afford to stop, couldn't afford to show any weakness. The Black Knights were still out there, and as long as they were, the war would rage on.

As the night dragged on, Jasmine found herself alone in the safehouse, the weight of everything pressing down on her. She stared at the bloodstained floor where Big Moe had fallen, the reality of her decisions settling over her like a dark cloud.

She'd made her choice, and there was no going back. But it was getting harder to ignore the doubts, the fear that maybe she was losing control. The Black Knights were ruthless, but the real enemy was the doubt creeping into her own ranks.

Jasmine closed her eyes, letting out a shaky breath. She couldn't afford to let her guard down, not for a second. The war wasn't just with the Black Knights—it was with herself, with the darkness that threatened to consume her.

As she sat there, alone with her thoughts, a sense of finality settled over her. She knew this was only the beginning. The war would escalate, more blood would be spilled, and the line between friend and enemy would blur even further.

But Jasmine was ready.

She had to be.

Because there was no other way out of this.

And as she looked out the window, into the dark streets that had shaped her, she knew one thing for sure—she would do whatever it took to survive.

Even if it meant losing everything in the process.

Chapter 5: Allies and Enemies

The dimly lit backroom of The Pit, a notorious underground club known for its dangerous clientele, was thick with smoke and tension. Jasmine sat at the table, her eyes sharp, scanning the faces around her. She was surrounded by some of the most feared figures in the city—men and women who had carved out their own empires in blood and hustle. But tonight, they were all here for one reason: to decide if they were gonna ride with Jasmine or against her.

The room was silent, save for the low hum of conversation leaking through the walls from the club outside. Jasmine's fingers tapped a rhythm on the table, her mind racing. She knew she needed these alliances—her war with the Black Knights was escalating, and she couldn't afford to fight it alone. But she also knew that trusting anyone in this room could be a fatal mistake.

The first to speak was King Solomon, an older man with a reputation for ruthlessness, his voice gravelly from years of chain-smoking. "Jas, you know I respect what you've built. But you askin' us to go to war with the Black Knights? That's a big ask, girl. What's in it for us?"

Jasmine leaned forward, her eyes locking onto Solomon's. "Respect, Solomon. You roll with me, and we take down the Black Knights, you get a piece of everything they got. Money, turf, connections—all of it. But more than that, you send a message that ain't nobody untouchable in this city."

Solomon nodded slowly, considering her words. "And what about after? What happens when they're gone? You planning to take it all for yourself?"

Jasmine smirked, though there was no humor in it. "Ain't nobody takin' nothin' from nobody. We divide it up fair. You get your share, I get mine. This ain't about greed, Solomon. This is about survival. You with me or not?"

Before Solomon could answer, a voice cut through the tension like a knife. "What's stoppin' us from just takin' you out right now and keepin' the shit for ourselves?"

Jasmine turned her gaze to the source—a woman named Nia, known on the streets as the Black Widow, a title earned from the countless men who had crossed her and ended up in the morgue. Nia was a wild card, dangerous and unpredictable, and Jasmine knew she had to tread carefully.

"Nia, you smart enough to know that takin' me out don't solve your problems. It just makes you a bigger target. The Black Knights come for you next, and you ain't got nobody to back you up. This ain't just about me—it's about all of us keepin' what we built," Jasmine replied, her tone cool and calculated.

Nia stared at Jasmine, her eyes narrowing, but she didn't say anything more. Jasmine took that as a good sign.

"Look, we all in this game for a reason," Jasmine continued, her voice steady and confident. "We built our empires from nothin', but we all know how fast it can fall apart. The Black Knights? They think they own these streets. They think they can take what's ours and leave us with scraps. I'm sayin' we flip the script on them. We hit 'em where it hurts and take back what's ours."

There was a murmur of agreement from around the table, but Jasmine knew better than to trust it. These people were only loyal as long as it benefited them, and she had to make sure the benefits were crystal clear.

King Solomon finally nodded, his expression thoughtful. "Alright, Jasmine. I'm in. But don't think for a second that I'm doin' this outta the goodness of my heart. We take the Black Knights down, and I want my cut, no questions asked."

"Same here," Nia added, her voice icy. "But if you cross me, Jas, I'll bury you myself."

Jasmine met her gaze without flinching. "I ain't gonna cross nobody. We in this together, for better or worse."

As the meeting broke up and the room emptied out, Jasmine stayed behind, her mind buzzing with the implications of what had just happened. She'd secured the alliances she needed, but she couldn't shake the feeling that something was off. These new allies—they weren't just in it for the money. They had their own agendas, and Jasmine knew she had to stay one step ahead if she was gonna survive.

Marcus walked over, his face as stoic as ever. "That went better than I expected, but I don't trust 'em. Solomon, Nia... they playin' their own game."

Jasmine nodded, her thoughts already turning to how she could use that to her advantage. "I know. They think they can play me, but I'mma make sure they know who's really in charge. We gotta keep 'em close, but we watch 'em. Any sign of them crossin' us, and we take 'em out. No hesitation."

Marcus looked at her, a flicker of concern in his eyes. "You ready for that, Jas? It's one thing to take out enemies. It's another to turn on your own people."

Jasmine's jaw tightened, the weight of her decisions pressing down on her. "Ain't nobody my people if they cross me, Marcus. You know that. This is war, and in war, you do what you gotta do."

Marcus nodded, but Jasmine could see the doubt lingering in his eyes. She couldn't afford to dwell on it, though. Not with so much at stake.

"Let's get outta here," Jasmine said, pushing herself to her feet. "We got work to do."

Jasmine and Marcus left The Pit, stepping out into the cold night air. The city around them was alive with the sounds of traffic, distant sirens, and the hum of a world that never slept. Jasmine pulled her coat tighter around her, her mind already racing ahead to what needed to be done.

But as they walked down the dimly lit street, Jasmine couldn't shake the feeling that they were being watched. Her instincts, honed by years of surviving in the streets, were screaming at her to be on high alert.

"Marcus," Jasmine murmured, her voice low. "You feel that?"

Marcus nodded, his eyes scanning their surroundings. "Yeah. Somethin' ain't right."

They kept walking, their pace steady but alert, every nerve on edge. The street was too quiet, too empty, and that set off all kinds of alarms in Jasmine's mind.

Suddenly, the sound of footsteps echoed behind them, quick and deliberate. Jasmine spun around, her hand going to her gun, but it was too late. A group of men emerged from the shadows, their faces obscured by hoods, their guns already drawn.

"Shit," Marcus hissed, his gun coming up fast.

Jasmine didn't wait for them to make the first move. She fired, the shot ringing out in the night, and all hell broke loose. The men returned fire, bullets tearing through the air as Jasmine and Marcus dove for cover behind a parked car.

"Ambush!" Jasmine shouted, her voice barely audible over the gunfire. She cursed under her breath—she should have known someone would try to pull this shit.

They exchanged fire, the sound of bullets hitting metal and shattering glass filling the night. Jasmine's heart pounded in her chest, her mind racing as she tried to figure out who had set this up. Was it the Black Knights? Or had one of her new "allies" decided to make their move early?

"Marcus, we gotta get outta here!" Jasmine yelled, her voice edged with urgency. They were pinned down, and it was only a matter of time before they were outgunned.

"Cover me!" Marcus shouted back, and Jasmine nodded, firing off a few more shots to keep the attackers at bay as Marcus made a break for a nearby alley.

Jasmine followed him, ducking down as bullets whizzed past her head. They reached the alley, and Jasmine could feel her heart pounding as they raced through the narrow passageways, trying to put as much distance between them and the ambush as possible.

When they finally stopped, panting and out of breath, Jasmine leaned against the wall, her mind still racing. "That was too damn close."

"Somebody set us up, Jas," Marcus said, his voice dark. "Ain't no way that was a coincidence."

Jasmine nodded, her eyes narrowing. "I know. And we gonna find out who it was."

But as they stood there, catching their breath, Jasmine couldn't shake the feeling that things were spiraling out of control. The alliances she'd made—they were supposed to make her stronger, but now it seemed like they were only making her more vulnerable.

As she looked out into the dark streets, Jasmine knew one thing for sure—there were no real allies in this game. Only enemies waiting for the right moment to strike.

And she was gonna have to figure out who to trust before it was too late.

Chapter 6: Escalation

The city felt like it was holding its breath, waiting for something to break. Jasmine could feel it in the air, the tension so thick it pressed against her chest, making it hard to breathe. The streets, usually alive with the hustle of the game, were quieter than usual. People stayed inside, eyes peeking out from behind curtains, knowing that something big was about to go down.

Jasmine sat in the backseat of the blacked-out SUV, her fingers drumming against the armrest as they rolled through the neighborhood. Marcus was driving, his eyes sharp, constantly scanning the streets for any sign of trouble. Tasha sat beside her, checking her gun for the third time.

"This shit's about to blow, Jas," Tasha muttered, her voice low. "I can feel it. Black Knights ain't gonna just let us keep pushin'. They gonna come at us with everything they got."

"I know," Jasmine replied, her voice tight. She leaned back in her seat, trying to keep her mind focused. "That's why we gotta be ready. We hit 'em first, hit 'em hard. Ain't no time for second-guessing."

Marcus nodded from the front seat. "I got the crew on standby. Everyone's strapped and ready to move when you give the word."

Jasmine stared out the window, the familiar streets blurring as they passed by. This was her home, her turf, but it felt different now—like the ground beneath her feet was shifting, ready to swallow her whole. She couldn't afford to lose control, not now. The Black Knights had taken too much already, and she wasn't about to let them take anything else.

"Pull over here," Jasmine ordered suddenly, her eyes locking onto a small park where kids usually played. It was empty now, the swings creaking in the breeze, an eerie reminder of what was at stake.

Marcus did as she said, parking the SUV at the curb. Jasmine got out, the cool air hitting her face like a slap. She walked over to the swings, her footsteps heavy, the weight of everything pressing down on her.

"This ain't just about us, y'know," Jasmine said quietly, more to herself than to Tasha and Marcus, who had followed her. "This war... it's spilling over. Kids, families... they caught up in this, and they don't even know why."

Tasha stepped closer, her expression softening. "Jas, this life... it ain't fair. It ain't never been. But we gotta do what we gotta do. You started this for a reason, and we all knew the risks."

Jasmine nodded, her eyes still on the empty playground. "Yeah... but that don't make it any easier."

The Black Knights didn't give Jasmine much time to dwell on her thoughts. The first strike came later that night, sudden and brutal. Word came through the network that one of their safehouses had been hit—hard. By the time Jasmine and her crew arrived, the place was a wreck, the air thick with smoke and the stench of blood.

Jasmine stepped over the bodies of her fallen soldiers, her heart pounding with rage and grief. The Black Knights had made their move, and it was a declaration of war written in blood.

"Fuck!" Tasha cursed, kicking over a broken chair in frustration. "They hit us bad, Jas. We lost a lot of good people."

Jasmine didn't respond, her mind racing as she surveyed the damage. This was more than just a hit—this was a message. The Black Knights were done playing around. They were coming for her, for everything she had left.

"We gotta hit back," Marcus said, his voice calm but laced with anger. "Hit 'em where it hurts, make 'em bleed."

Jasmine nodded, her jaw set in determination. "We will. But we ain't just gonna react. We gonna take the fight to them, on our terms."

Jasmine's plan was simple: draw the Black Knights into a trap and wipe them out in one fell swoop. She knew where they'd be—another one of their stash houses, heavily guarded but vulnerable if hit from the right angles. It was risky, but Jasmine was done playing it safe.

The night was dark, the kind of darkness that swallowed sound and made everything feel more intense. Jasmine and her crew moved through the streets like shadows, their guns ready, their eyes sharp. They split into teams, surrounding the building from all sides, cutting off any chance of escape.

"On my mark," Jasmine whispered into the comms, her heart pounding in her chest. "Three... two... one... go!"

The silence exploded into chaos as Jasmine's crew hit the stash house from all sides. Gunfire erupted, the sound deafening in the narrow streets, bullets ripping through the night. The Black Knights were caught off guard, scrambling to defend their turf, but Jasmine's crew was relentless, pushing them back with brutal efficiency.

Jasmine moved through the chaos like a force of nature, her gun spitting fire, her mind cold and focused. She didn't flinch as bodies dropped around her, didn't hesitate as she cleared room after room. The Black Knights were outmatched, outgunned, and they knew it.

But just as it seemed like they had the upper hand, the sound of approaching sirens cut through the noise. Jasmine's heart skipped a beat—cops. The last thing she needed was the law getting involved, especially with bodies on the ground and guns in their hands.

"Wrap it up!" Jasmine shouted, her voice cutting through the comms. "We gotta move, now!"

Marcus and Tasha started pulling the crew out, but the damage had already been done. As Jasmine made her way to the exit, she caught sight of a young boy, no older than ten, cowering in a corner, his eyes wide with fear.

"Fuck," Jasmine muttered under her breath, her heart clenching. She hadn't known there were civilians in the building, but it didn't change the reality of the situation. This wasn't just a war between gangs—it was tearing apart the very fabric of the neighborhood.

She grabbed the boy, pulling him to his feet. "Come on, we gotta get you outta here."

The boy didn't resist, too scared to do anything but follow her lead. As they made their way out of the building, Jasmine could hear the wails of mothers, the cries of children, the chaos spilling out into the streets. This wasn't just about her anymore. It was about everyone who lived here, everyone who was caught in the crossfire.

Back at the safehouse, the weight of the night's events pressed down on Jasmine like a ton of bricks. The ambush had been successful, but at what cost? The violence was escalating, and it was spreading like a virus, infecting everything it touched.

Tasha sat beside her, her expression dark. "Jas, this shit's gettin' outta hand. We can't keep doin' this. People... innocent people are gettin' hurt."

"I know," Jasmine replied, her voice hollow. "But we can't stop now. If we back down, the Black Knights win. They take everything we got."

"But at what cost?" Tasha demanded, her eyes flashing with anger. "We supposed to be protectin' this neighborhood, not destroyin' it."

Jasmine didn't have an answer for that. She knew Tasha was right, but she couldn't see a way out. The war had taken on a life of its own, and now it was devouring everything in its path.

Marcus joined them, his face grim. "We hit 'em hard tonight, but they gonna hit back. This ain't over, Jas. Not by a long shot."

Jasmine nodded, the weight of her decisions pressing down on her like never before. She'd started this war to protect what was hers, to avenge her mother, but now... now it was spiraling out of control.

As she sat there, the sounds of the night filtering through the windows, Jasmine couldn't shake the feeling that she was losing herself in the process. The streets had shaped her, made her who she was, but now they were threatening to consume her whole.

The war wasn't just with the Black Knights anymore—it was with herself, with the darkness that was creeping ever closer, threatening to swallow her whole.

But there was no turning back now.

The only way out was through.

And Jasmine was prepared to see it through to the bitter end, no matter what it cost her.

Chapter 7: Marcus's Secrets

The sun hung low over the city, casting long shadows across the streets as Jasmine made her way back to the safehouse. The day had been brutal—more skirmishes, more bloodshed—and the weight of it all was beginning to wear on her. But something else had been gnawing at her, a feeling she couldn't quite shake. It was Marcus. He'd been acting different, distant, like he was hiding something. Jasmine couldn't put her finger on it, but she knew something wasn't right.

As she stepped into the dimly lit room, she found Marcus already there, leaning against the wall, staring out the window with a look that was hard to read. Jasmine felt a pang of unease in her chest. She wanted to trust him—after all, he was her right-hand, her brother in this war—but doubt had a way of creeping in, especially in a game as dirty as this one.

"Long day," Marcus muttered without turning around, his voice flat.

"Yeah," Jasmine replied, her eyes narrowing as she studied him. "What's on your mind?"

Marcus finally turned to face her, his expression unreadable. "Just thinkin' 'bout the moves we gotta make next. This war ain't lettin' up, Jas. We gotta stay sharp."

Jasmine nodded, but she couldn't shake the feeling that there was something more to it. Marcus had always been the steady one, the rock she could lean on, but lately, he seemed off—distracted, almost secretive. She opened her mouth to say something, but the words caught in her throat. How could she question him when he'd been by her side through everything?

"Yeah," she said instead, forcing a smile. "We'll get through this. We always do."

But the doubt lingered, like a dark cloud that refused to lift.

The next few days passed in a blur of violence and chaos, the war with the Black Knights consuming every waking moment. But even amidst the bloodshed, Jasmine couldn't ignore the nagging feeling that something was wrong with Marcus. He was always there, but somehow, it felt like he was slipping away, like he was keeping secrets.

It wasn't just his behavior, either. Jasmine had started hearing whispers—little things that didn't add up. She'd caught him on the phone late at night, his voice low and tense, conversations that ended abruptly when she walked into the room. And then there were the meetings—quick, covert meet-ups with people Jasmine didn't recognize, people who weren't part of their circle.

One night, after a particularly brutal skirmish, Jasmine decided she couldn't take it anymore. She had to know what was going on, had to figure out if the man she'd trusted with her life was still on her side. So she did something she never thought she'd do—she followed him.

It wasn't hard to track him through the city. Marcus knew the streets better than anyone, but Jasmine knew him. She kept her distance, sticking to the shadows as he made his way to a rundown building on the edge of their territory. The place was a dump, half-collapsed and reeking of rot, but Marcus didn't hesitate as he slipped inside.

Jasmine's heart pounded in her chest as she crept closer, her mind racing. What the hell was Marcus doing here? And who was he meeting? She crouched by a broken window, peering inside just in time to see Marcus talking to a man she didn't recognize—tall, lean, with a face that spoke of danger.

The conversation was heated, their voices low but intense. Jasmine strained to hear, catching snippets of words that made her blood run cold.

"...can't keep doin' this... she'll find out..."

"...no choice... gotta make a move soon..."

Jasmine's heart sank as the realization hit her like a punch to the gut. Marcus was hiding something—something big. And whatever it was, it involved betraying her.

Jasmine's mind raced as she made her way back to the safehouse, her thoughts a whirlwind of anger, betrayal, and confusion. She couldn't believe it—Marcus, the one person she thought she could trust, was plotting behind her back. But why? And what the hell was he planning?

By the time she reached the safehouse, her hands were trembling with rage. She couldn't let this slide—she needed answers, and she needed them now. Marcus was there, sitting at the table with Tasha, talking in low tones. Jasmine stormed in, her eyes blazing.

"Tasha, give us a minute," Jasmine snapped, her voice like ice.

Tasha looked between them, her eyes narrowing in concern. "Jas, what's going on?"

"Now, Tasha," Jasmine repeated, her tone leaving no room for argument.

Tasha hesitated, then nodded, shooting a worried glance at Marcus before leaving the room. As soon as the door closed behind her, Jasmine turned on Marcus, her anger boiling over.

"You wanna tell me what the fuck's going on, Marcus?" Jasmine demanded, her voice trembling with barely restrained fury.

Marcus looked up at her, surprise flickering across his face. "What you talkin' about, Jas?"

"Don't play dumb with me!" Jasmine shouted, slamming her hands down on the table. "I know you been meetin' with people outside the crew. I heard you, Marcus. What the fuck are you planning?"

Marcus's eyes hardened, his expression closing off. "You don't know what you talkin' about, Jas. You paranoid. This war's got you seein' ghosts."

"Don't lie to me!" Jasmine yelled, her voice cracking. "You think I don't know when someone's tryin' to play me? I've seen it all before, Marcus. I trusted you, and now you doin' this? Behind my back?"

Marcus stood up slowly, his eyes never leaving hers. "You don't know shit, Jas. You think this war's just 'bout takin' out the Black Knights? It's bigger than that. You ain't the only one with skin in the game."

Jasmine's heart pounded in her chest, the anger and hurt twisting inside her like a knife. "Then tell me! Tell me what the hell's goin' on, Marcus!"

But Marcus just shook his head, his expression unreadable. "I can't, Jas. Not yet. You ain't ready."

"Ready?" Jasmine spat, her voice dripping with venom. "You think I'm weak? You think I can't handle it? After everything we been through, you still don't trust me?"

Marcus sighed, running a hand over his face. "It ain't 'bout trust, Jas. It's 'bout protectin' you. You think I don't know what you're feelin'? But some things... some things you can't just jump into. You gotta be smart."

Jasmine stared at him, the anger and confusion warring inside her. She didn't know what to believe anymore. Marcus had been by her side through everything, but now... now she didn't know if she could trust him.

"You better figure out what side you on, Marcus," Jasmine said, her voice cold. "Cause if you ain't with me, you against me. And I ain't gonna hesitate to take you out if you cross me."

Marcus didn't flinch, his expression hard. "You do what you gotta do, Jas. But don't make a move you gonna regret."

The tension between them lingered like a bad taste in Jasmine's mouth. She couldn't shake the feeling that everything was spiraling out of control, that the war was tearing apart the very foundation she'd built. Marcus was keeping secrets, and now she didn't know who she could trust.

Over the next few days, she kept a close eye on him, watching for any sign that he was planning something. But Marcus was good—too good. He went about his business as usual, but Jasmine could see the cracks in the facade, the moments when his mask slipped and she caught a glimpse of the man beneath.

But the more she watched, the more questions she had. Who was that man Marcus had met with? And what was he planning? Jasmine knew she needed answers, but she also knew that pushing Marcus too hard could backfire. She was playing a dangerous game, and one wrong move could cost her everything.

As she lay awake at night, the weight of her decisions pressing down on her, Jasmine couldn't shake the feeling that the walls were closing in. The war with the Black Knights was reaching a breaking point, and now, the one person she'd thought she could rely on was slipping through her fingers.

She had to be careful. She had to be smart.

Because in this game, trust was a luxury she couldn't afford.

And Marcus... Marcus was a wild card that could either save her or destroy her.

But one way or another, Jasmine was going to find out the truth.

Even if it killed her.

Chapter 8: Personal Fallout

The streets were quieter than usual, but Jasmine knew it was just the calm before the storm. The war with the Black Knights was escalating, and the tension was creeping into every part of her life. She pulled up outside Malik's spot, her little brother's new place after he'd moved out on his own. She hadn't seen him much since things started getting heavy, but she needed to check in, to make sure he was okay.

She knocked on the door, and after a few moments, Malik opened it, his face hard and closed off. He was only sixteen, but he'd seen more than most men twice his age. Jasmine could see the anger in his eyes, the same anger that burned in her own heart.

"Hey, Malik," Jasmine said, trying to keep her voice light, but even she could hear the strain in it.

"What you want, Jas?" Malik asked, not bothering to hide the edge in his voice.

Jasmine sighed, stepping inside without waiting for an invitation. "I just wanted to check on you, see how you holdin' up."

Malik snorted, shaking his head. "Check on me? Really, Jas? You think I need checkin' on? I'm out here, same as you, tryin' to survive. But you too busy playin' queen of the streets to give a damn 'bout what's happenin' to your own blood."

The words stung, but Jasmine forced herself to stay calm. "Malik, I ain't playin' nothin'. I'm out here fightin' to keep us safe. You know what these streets are like. You think I wanted this? You think I wanted to drag you into it?"

Malik's eyes flashed with anger. "You didn't have to drag me into shit, Jas! I'm in it whether I like it or not. And now, everywhere I go, people lookin' at me like I'm some kinda prince or somethin', just 'cause of who my sister is. But you don't even see it, do you? You don't see how this shit is tearin' us apart."

Jasmine swallowed hard, the guilt weighing heavy on her chest. "Malik, I'm sorry. I didn't want this for you. I didn't want this for any of us. But it's too late now. We gotta stick together, watch each other's backs."

Malik looked at her, his expression softening just a bit, but the anger was still there, simmering beneath the surface. "Maybe. But you better start thinkin' about what really matters, Jas. Before you lose everything."

Jasmine didn't have an answer to that, so she just nodded, feeling the weight of his words settle in her gut like a stone. She'd already lost so much—her mother, her sense of peace—and now, she was on the brink of losing the only family she had left.

Later that night, Jasmine found herself in familiar territory, but the comfort she once found here was fading. Cal's apartment was dimly lit, the shadows playing tricks with her mind. Cal was leaning against the kitchen counter, a bottle of Henny in one hand, his eyes narrowed as he watched her.

"You been quiet, Jas," Cal said, his voice low and smooth, but there was an edge to it, something dangerous lurking beneath the surface. "What's goin' on in that head of yours?"

Jasmine shrugged, trying to play it off, but the tension was thick between them. "Just got a lot on my mind, Cal. You know how it is."

Cal nodded, but his eyes never left hers. "Yeah, I know. But it feels like you been driftin'. Like you here, but you ain't really here, y'know?"

Jasmine turned away, not wanting to meet his gaze. "I got a lot goin' on. The Black Knights, the crew... Malik. It's all a mess right now."

Cal pushed off the counter, moving closer to her, his presence heavy and intoxicating. "You think you the only one with shit to deal with? We all got problems, Jas. But when you start keepin' secrets, that's when things go wrong."

Jasmine tensed, the accusation in his words cutting deep. "What you talkin' 'bout, Cal?"

Cal's eyes flashed with something that looked like jealousy, but there was more to it—something darker. "You think I don't see it? You think I don't know 'bout Marcus, 'bout how close y'all been lately?"

Jasmine's heart skipped a beat, a cold dread settling in her stomach. "Marcus? He's my right-hand, Cal. Ain't nothin' goin' on between us."

Cal's expression didn't soften. "Maybe not. But he been actin' real shady, and you ain't even noticed, have you? You so caught up in this war, you don't even see what's happenin' right under your nose."

Jasmine felt a surge of anger, a defensive reflex kicking in. "Marcus ain't your business, Cal. And neither is mine. You think you can come at me with that shit, try to make me doubt my own crew?"

Cal stepped closer, his voice dropping to a dangerous whisper. "I'm just tryin' to keep it real, Jas. You need to open your eyes before it's too late. Ain't nobody out here you can trust, not even the ones closest to you."

Jasmine's anger flared, but beneath it was a flicker of fear, of doubt. She didn't want to admit it, but Cal's words hit too close to home. She was losing control, losing sight of what mattered, and now, the people she cared about most were slipping through her fingers.

She pushed past him, needing to put some distance between them, needing to clear her head. "I need some air."

Cal didn't try to stop her, but his voice followed her to the door, low and filled with something that sounded almost like regret. "You better figure this out, Jas. Before you lose everything."

Jasmine walked the streets, the cold night air biting at her skin, but it did little to cool the fire burning inside her. Cal's words echoed in her mind, mixing with Malik's accusations, until she couldn't tell where the anger ended and the fear began.

She found herself back at the safehouse, the place that had become more like a prison than a refuge. Marcus was there, sitting at the table, his face illuminated by the harsh light of the overhead lamp. He looked up as she entered, something unreadable in his eyes.

"Jas, you okay?" he asked, but his voice was cautious, like he already knew the answer.

Jasmine didn't sit down. She couldn't. The tension in her chest was too tight, too suffocating. "Marcus, we need to talk."

Marcus's eyes narrowed slightly, but he didn't move. "What's goin' on?"

Jasmine took a deep breath, trying to steady herself. "I need to know what's been goin' on with you. Lately, you been distant, secretive. I know you got my back, but I need the truth, Marcus. Are you with me or not?"

Marcus didn't answer right away, and the silence stretched between them, thick and suffocating. When he finally spoke, his voice was low and controlled. "Jas, you know I'm with you. But you also know there's things I can't talk about. Things that ain't just 'bout you and me."

Jasmine's heart pounded in her chest, a mix of fear and frustration. "I need to trust you, Marcus. But right now, I'm startin' to doubt everything."

Marcus stood up, his expression hardening. "You think I'm gonna betray you, Jas? After everything we been through?"

Jasmine didn't back down. "I don't know what to think anymore. I got people whisperin' in my ear, tellin' me you ain't who I thought you were. And I need to know the truth."

Marcus's jaw clenched, the tension between them thick enough to cut. "You wanna know the truth? The truth is, this war's got us all twisted. We all playin' a dangerous game, and the lines are gettin' blurred. But I'm still here, Jas. I'm still standin' by your side."

Jasmine wanted to believe him, but the doubt was still there, gnawing at her insides. She didn't know what was real anymore, didn't know who she could trust. And the more she tried to hold on, the more everything seemed to slip away.

"I don't want to lose you, Marcus, not like I lost Dre" she whispered, the vulnerability in her voice surprising even herself.

Marcus softened, stepping closer. "You ain't gonna lose me, Jas. But you gotta trust me, just like I trust you. We in this together, for better or worse."

Jasmine nodded, but the unease still lingered. The war was tearing everything apart, and now, even her closest relationships were fraying at the edges. She didn't know how much longer she could keep it together, didn't know if she could survive the fallout.

But one thing was certain—whatever happened next, Jasmine was in it to the end.

And she would do whatever it took to make sure she didn't lose everything she'd fought for. Even if it meant making choices that would haunt her forever.

Chapter 9: The Turning Point

The night was dark, the kind of darkness that swallowed everything whole, leaving nothing but shadows and the distant hum of a city that never really slept. Jasmine stood on the rooftop of an abandoned building, looking down at the chaos below. Her crew had just pulled off the biggest hit of the war—taking out the Black Knights' main distribution hub. It was a bloodbath, bodies scattered like discarded trash, the air thick with the stench of death and burning rubber.

Jasmine's chest heaved with adrenaline, her mind racing as she watched her crew sweep through the wreckage, mopping up any stragglers. They'd won. They'd actually fucking won. The Black Knights were on the ropes now, their operations crippled, their soldiers scattered. And Jasmine? She was on the verge of securing her empire, the one she'd fought tooth and nail for.

But as she stood there, watching the flames lick at the sky, a cold knot tightened in her gut. This wasn't supposed to feel this way. Victory, after all this time, should've felt sweet, like the taste of freedom. But all Jasmine felt was hollow, like something vital had been ripped out of her and replaced with a gaping void.

Marcus appeared at her side, his face covered in grime and sweat, but his eyes were sharp. "We did it, Jas. They done. Ain't no comin' back from this."

Jasmine nodded, her voice caught in her throat. She wanted to celebrate, to let out the victory cry she'd been holding in for so long, but all she could manage was a half-hearted smile. "Yeah, we did it."

But even as the words left her mouth, they felt like ashes on her tongue. The cost had been too high, the blood too thick. She looked down at her hands, still trembling from the fight, and all she could see was the blood she'd spilled to get here.

"You good?" Marcus asked, his voice softer now, like he could sense the storm raging inside her.

"Yeah… I'm good," Jasmine lied, turning away from the scene below. But deep down, she knew she wasn't good. She was far from it.

Later that night, Jasmine found herself alone in a dingy motel room on the outskirts of the city. The bed was lumpy, the walls peeling, but she didn't care. It was quiet, and that was all she needed right now—some space to breathe, to think, to figure out what the hell she was feeling.

She sat on the edge of the bed, her mind replaying the events of the night over and over again. The violence, the bloodshed, the screams of the dying—all of it was still fresh in her mind, seared into her consciousness like a brand. She'd won, but at what cost? How many lives had she destroyed to get here? How much of herself had she lost along the way?

Jasmine's eyes drifted to the mirror on the wall, her reflection staring back at her, cold and distant. She barely recognized herself anymore—the hard lines of her face, the emptiness in her eyes. The girl she'd once been, the one who'd dreamed of something more, was long gone, buried under the weight of her choices.

She'd become something else, something darker, something twisted by the streets. And now, as she stood on the brink of victory, she couldn't help but wonder if it had all been worth it.

"Is this what you wanted, Ma?" Jasmine whispered to the empty room, her voice cracking with emotion. "Is this what you would've wanted for me?"

But there was no answer, only the silence that pressed down on her like a shroud. Her mother was gone, taken from her by the very life Jasmine had chosen to embrace. And now, as she looked back on everything she'd done, everything she'd sacrificed, she couldn't help but feel like she'd betrayed her mother's memory.

Jasmine clenched her fists, her nails digging into her palms until she drew blood. She couldn't afford to think like this, couldn't afford to second-guess herself now. She'd come too far, fought too hard to let doubt creep in. The Black Knights were almost finished, and she was so close to securing everything she'd ever wanted.

But deep down, a voice whispered that she was losing something far more valuable—her soul.

The next day, Jasmine was back in the city, her mind still reeling from the night before. The streets were buzzing with the news of the Black Knights' defeat—people whispering her name, talking about the power she'd amassed, the empire she was building. But Jasmine couldn't bring herself to care.

She walked through the neighborhood, the place she'd grown up in, the place she'd fought so hard to protect. But it didn't feel like home anymore. The people looked at her with a mix of fear and respect, but there was something else in their eyes, something that made Jasmine's stomach turn—disappointment.

She passed by the corner where kids used to play, now empty and silent. The old bodega, where she and Malik used to get snacks after school, was boarded up, the windows shattered. The war had torn through the community like a hurricane, leaving nothing but destruction in its wake. And Jasmine had been at the center of it all.

As she walked, she thought about Malik, about how distant he'd been lately. She hadn't seen him since their argument, and the guilt gnawed at her. She'd dragged him into this life, made him a part of her war, and now she was losing him too.

She stopped in front of the old church, the one her mother used to take them to when they were kids. The doors were still open, but the place was empty, the pews gathering dust. Jasmine hesitated, then walked inside, the silence wrapping around her like a blanket.

She sat down in the back, her mind racing. She'd won the battle, but the victory felt hollow. She was on the verge of securing her empire, but she couldn't shake the feeling that she was losing everything else that mattered.

She thought about Cal, about the tension that had grown between them, about the way he'd looked at her the last time they'd spoken. She thought about Marcus, about the secrets he was keeping, the doubt that had crept into their relationship. She thought about all the people she'd lost, all the lives she'd destroyed, and the weight of it all threatened to crush her.

Jasmine buried her face in her hands, fighting back the tears that burned in her eyes. She'd sacrificed so much to get here, but she couldn't help but wonder if she'd sacrificed the wrong things. She'd given up her humanity, her soul, and now she was left with nothing but ashes.

"Ma, I'm sorry," Jasmine whispered, her voice breaking. "I'm so sorry."

But there was no one to hear her, no one to offer comfort or forgiveness. She was alone, the empire she'd fought for crumbling around her. And for the first time, Jasmine didn't know if she had the strength to keep going.

As night fell, Jasmine found herself back on the streets, the city lights casting long shadows as she walked. Her phone buzzed with messages, her crew celebrating the victory, making plans for the future. But Jasmine felt disconnected, like she was watching it all from a distance.

She stopped at a street corner, looking out over the city she'd fought so hard to control. It was hers now, or at least it would be soon. But instead of pride, all she felt was a deep, aching emptiness.

The streets had given her power, but they'd taken everything else. And now, as she stood on the brink of victory, Jasmine couldn't shake the feeling that she'd lost something far more valuable.

But there was no turning back now. The war wasn't over, and there were still battles to be fought, still enemies to defeat. Jasmine had come too far to stop now, even if it meant losing herself in the process.

She took a deep breath, steeling herself for what was to come. The road ahead was dark, but Jasmine was ready to walk it, no matter where it led.

Because in the end, there was no other choice.

This was her life, her empire, and she would see it through to the bitter end—no matter the cost.

Chapter 10: The Trap is Set

The city was a beast that never slept, always hungry, always grinding. Marcus had learned to navigate its dark alleys and backrooms with a skill that came from years of surviving its worst. But now, as he moved through the familiar streets, there was an added layer to his game—a deception that cut deeper than any blade.

He glanced at his phone, the screen glowing with a message from his contact in the Feds. The plan was in motion, the pieces falling into place, and Marcus felt a cold, steady determination settle in his chest. He had a job to do, one that would end this war once and for all. But to do it, he had to betray the one person who trusted him the most.

As he slid into a nondescript sedan parked at the corner, a manila envelope already waiting on the passenger seat, Marcus felt the weight of his decision pressing down on him. The Feds had been tightening the noose around Jasmine's empire for months, and now, with Marcus on the inside, they were ready to make their move.

He opened the envelope, scanning the contents—documents, photos, details of every deal Jasmine had ever made, every person she'd ever trusted. The Feds wanted everything, and Marcus was the key. But as he stared at the evidence, a flicker of doubt gnawed at him. He'd made his choice, but that didn't make it any easier.

"Get your head in the game, Marcus," he muttered to himself, shoving the envelope into the glove compartment. There was no room for second-guessing, no time for regrets. He'd come too far, and the Feds had too much on him to back out now and he had to save himself.

He pulled out his burner phone, dialing a number he'd memorized. It rang twice before a gruff voice answered. "You got something for me?"

"Yeah," Marcus replied, his voice steady. "It's all set. Just make sure your people are ready when I give the signal."

The voice on the other end grunted in acknowledgment. "Good. Keep it clean, Marcus. You know what's at stake."

"I know," Marcus said, hanging up. He leaned back in the seat, closing his eyes for a moment. The trap was set, and now all he had to do was play his part, make sure Jasmine never saw it coming.

Back at the safehouse, Marcus slipped seamlessly into his role, the mask of loyalty firmly in place. The crew was gathered around, going over plans for the next hit, but Marcus had other ideas. He needed to create cracks, weaken the foundation, and it had to start from within.

He waited until the right moment, then spoke up, his voice calm but laced with just enough doubt to plant the seed. "Jas, I been thinkin'. We might be movin' too fast. Black Knights might be down, but they ain't out. We push too hard, we might be walkin' into a trap."

Jasmine looked up from the map spread out on the table, her eyes narrowing. "What you talkin' 'bout, Marcus? We got 'em on the ropes. Now's the time to finish this."

Marcus nodded, keeping his tone measured. "I feel you, but we ain't the only ones in this game. Word on the street is some of our people been gettin' sloppy. Cops been sniffin' around, askin' questions. We gotta be careful."

Tasha, who'd been listening quietly, chimed in, her voice tinged with worry. "Marcus might be right, Jas. We ain't invincible. Maybe we should lay low, regroup."

Jasmine's expression hardened, the pressure of leadership weighing on her. "We lay low, we lose momentum. The Black Knights ain't gonna give us no breaks. We gotta stay on the offensive."

But the doubt had already been sown, the tension in the room thickening as Marcus's words lingered in the air. He could see it in their faces—the uncertainty, the fear. It was subtle, but it was enough. Enough to make them second-guess, to hesitate when they needed to be decisive.

"Just thinkin' 'bout the long game, Jas," Marcus added, his tone softening. "I got your back, always. But I don't wanna see us go down 'cause we didn't play it smart."

Jasmine studied him for a long moment, her instincts warring with the trust she'd placed in him. Finally, she nodded, but her eyes were shadowed with doubt. "Aight, Marcus. We'll tighten things up, make sure we ain't takin' no unnecessary risks. But we keep movin'. We ain't stoppin' now."

Marcus nodded, satisfaction coiling in his chest. The cracks were forming, just like he'd planned. Now, it was only a matter of time.

Later that night, Marcus made another move, one that would push things closer to the breaking point. He arranged a meeting with one of Jasmine's suppliers, a mid-level dealer named Mario who was always looking out for himself. Mario was the weak link, the one Marcus knew he could manipulate.

They met in a dark alley, the kind of place where deals were made and lives were ended. Mario was nervous, his eyes darting around as he approached. "Marcus, what's this 'bout? I ain't lookin' for no trouble."

Marcus kept his expression neutral, his tone cold. "Ain't no trouble, Mario. Just business. But I need you to do somethin' for me."

Mario swallowed hard, his nerves showing. "What you need?"

Marcus stepped closer, lowering his voice. "You keep your mouth shut and your head down, but when the time comes, you fall back. Let things play out. Ain't nobody gonna know it was you. And when it's over, you get your cut, no questions asked."

Mario hesitated, his fear palpable. "And if I say no?"

Marcus's eyes hardened, his tone deadly. "You ain't sayin' no, Mario. You ain't got no choice. You cross me, and you know what happens. I ain't gotta spell it out."

Mario nodded quickly, his face pale. "Aight, Marcus. I'm in. But you better keep your word."

Marcus smirked, the satisfaction of control settling in his bones. "You just do what I say, and you'll be fine."

As Mario slunk away, Marcus felt a dark thrill of power. The pieces were falling into place, and soon, Jasmine's empire would come crashing down, and she wouldn't even see it coming.

The next day, Marcus made sure to be by Jasmine's side, playing his role to perfection. They were in a meeting with their top lieutenants, going over the plans for their final push against the Black Knights. Jasmine was focused, her mind sharp as she laid out the strategy, but Marcus was already thinking ahead, already planning the final move.

He waited for the right moment, then leaned in, his voice low and confidential. "Jas, I been workin' on somethin' that might give us an edge. A new contact, someone who's got info on the Black Knights' next move. We hit them before they hit us, we end this once and for all."

Jasmine looked intrigued, but cautious. "Who's this contact?"

Marcus shook his head, playing the part of the loyal soldier. "Someone who don't wanna be known. But the info's solid. I can set up a meet, make sure it's legit."

Jasmine considered it, her instincts telling her to be wary, but Marcus had never steered her wrong before. "Aight. Set it up. But I wanna be there. No more surprises."

Marcus nodded, a smirk tugging at the corner of his lips. "You got it, Jas. We'll make sure everything's in place."

But as they made their plans, Marcus knew that the meeting was the final piece of the puzzle. He'd lead Jasmine right into the trap, and when the time came, he'd watch it all burn. The Feds would swoop in, take her down, and Marcus would walk away clean, his hands washed of the blood and betrayal.

The end was coming, and Jasmine didn't even see it.

But Marcus did.

And he was ready to pull the trigger.

Chapter 11: The Raid

The night was eerily quiet, too quiet, as if the city itself was holding its breath. Jasmine sat in the safehouse, a grim sense of foreboding creeping over her. She couldn't shake the feeling that something was off. The streets had been too calm lately, like the eye of a storm, and Jasmine knew better than to trust the silence.

Marcus was by her side, as always, his face a mask of calm. But there was something in his eyes, something that made Jasmine's stomach twist with unease. She'd noticed it more and more lately, a flicker of something she couldn't quite place. But every time she tried to push it away, to focus on the war at hand, the feeling would come back stronger.

"Jas, you good?" Marcus asked, his voice breaking through her thoughts.

Jasmine forced a smile, pushing the unease down. "Yeah, I'm good. Just got a lot on my mind."

Marcus nodded, his eyes unreadable. "We all do. But tonight's gonna be big. We gotta stay sharp."

Jasmine nodded, but the feeling of dread gnawed at her. She couldn't shake the sense that something was coming, something she wasn't ready for.

The first sign that something was wrong came in the form of a loud crash, the sound of doors being kicked in, followed by shouts and the unmistakable crack of gunfire. Jasmine's heart leaped into her throat as she sprang to her feet, grabbing her gun from the table.

"Shit! What the fuck is goin' on?" Tasha screamed, rushing into the room, her eyes wide with fear.

Jasmine didn't have time to answer. The safehouse, their stronghold, was under attack, and it wasn't just any attack. The precision, the timing—it was too coordinated, too perfect. This wasn't the Black Knights. This was something bigger.

"They're here! Move! Now!" Jasmine shouted, her voice cutting through the chaos as she led the charge out of the room. Her crew was already in disarray, scrambling to grab weapons, to find cover, but it was too late.

As they burst out into the main room, Jasmine's worst fears were confirmed. The Feds had hit them, and they'd hit them hard. The windows shattered as tear gas canisters were tossed inside, the air thick with smoke and the acrid smell of chemicals. Red and blue lights flashed outside, the sound of sirens growing louder as the walls closed in.

"Feds!" Marcus yelled, his voice full of urgency. "They got us boxed in!"

Jasmine's mind raced, adrenaline pumping through her veins as she tried to make sense of the situation. How the fuck had they known? How had they gotten the drop on them like this?

But there was no time for questions. The Feds were moving in, a wall of bodies in tactical gear, guns drawn, faces hidden behind masks. Jasmine fired off a few shots, the sound of gunfire deafening in the enclosed space, but she knew it was a losing battle.

"Back! Get to the back!" Jasmine ordered, trying to regroup her crew, but the panic had already set in. People were running in all directions, the sense of order crumbling as the Feds closed in from every side.

"Jas, we gotta move! We can't stay here!" Marcus shouted, grabbing her arm and pulling her toward the back exit.

Jasmine hesitated, the weight of everything crashing down on her. This was it. Everything she'd built, everything she'd fought for, was falling apart right in front of her. But Marcus was right—they had to move. If they stayed, they'd all be dead or in cuffs within minutes.

"Go!" Jasmine yelled, shoving Tasha and a few others toward the door. "Get outta here! Now!"

The back alley was dark and narrow, the perfect place to make a quick getaway. But the Feds were everywhere, their presence choking the streets. Jasmine and Marcus led the way, ducking behind dumpsters, slipping through shadows, trying to stay one step ahead of the law.

"Jas, this way!" Marcus called, motioning toward a side street that led deeper into the maze of alleys.

Jasmine followed, her heart pounding in her chest, her mind racing. They needed to regroup, find a safe place to hole up, but every option felt like a trap. The Feds were too close, their net tightening around her with every passing second.

As they rounded a corner, Jasmine spotted a van parked haphazardly, its driver's side door open, engine still running. It was their only chance.

"Get in!" Jasmine ordered, shoving Marcus toward the van. He didn't hesitate, jumping into the driver's seat and slamming the door as Jasmine and the others piled in.

Marcus floored the gas, the tires screeching as they tore down the alley, the van lurching forward with a jolt. Jasmine glanced out the back window, her breath catching as she saw the Feds swarming behind them, their faces lit by the flashing lights, guns drawn.

"Fuck!" Tasha cursed, her voice shaky. "How the hell did they find us, Jas? How?"

Jasmine didn't have an answer. All she knew was that they were in deep shit, and the walls were closing in fast.

As they sped through the streets, the realization hit Jasmine like a freight train. This wasn't just bad luck. This wasn't just a random raid. Someone had set them up. Someone had known exactly where they'd be, exactly when to strike.

Her mind flashed back to Marcus, to the conversations they'd had, to the way he'd seemed so calm, so in control. And then it hit her—like a punch to the gut.

"Marcus," Jasmine whispered, the word slipping out before she could stop it.

Marcus glanced at her in the rearview mirror, his expression unreadable. "What?"

Jasmine's heart pounded, her thoughts racing. It all made sense now. The warnings, the hesitation, the sudden appearance of the Feds. Marcus had been playing her all along.

"You did this," Jasmine hissed, her voice low and dangerous. "You fucking set us up."

The tension in the van snapped like a rubber band, everyone going deadly silent as they realized what Jasmine was saying.

Marcus didn't deny it. His grip tightened on the steering wheel, his jaw clenched. "Jas, I had no choice. They had me. It was either this, or we all go down."

Jasmine's vision blurred with rage, her hands shaking as she reached for her gun. "You sold us out, Marcus. You fucking sold me out."

Marcus swerved the van sharply, avoiding a parked car as he tried to keep control. "I did what I had to do, Jas. You think this was easy? You think I wanted this?"

Jasmine's finger itched on the trigger, but she hesitated, the weight of their history pressing down on her. Marcus had been her right hand, her brother. And now he was the reason her empire was crumbling.

Tasha's voice broke through the tension, shaky and full of fear. "Jas, we gotta get outta here. This ain't the time."

Jasmine's eyes locked on Marcus's in the mirror, a storm of emotions swirling between them. But she knew Tasha was right. They were out of time, out of options.

"Drive," Jasmine finally said, her voice cold. "But when this is over, you're gonna pay for what you did, Marcus. I promise you that."

Marcus didn't respond, his focus on the road, but the unspoken understanding was clear. The bond they'd shared was shattered, and there was no going back.

As they tore through the city, Jasmine watched the streets fly by, her mind reeling from the betrayal, from the realization that everything she'd built was slipping away. The Feds were everywhere, the city alive with sirens and flashing lights, the air thick with the sense of finality.

Her empire was crumbling, the walls she'd built to protect herself and her people falling apart piece by piece. Key players were being arrested, eliminated, the foundation she'd fought so hard to build turning to dust beneath her feet.

But the rage inside her wouldn't die, wouldn't let her give up. She was going to survive this, no matter what. She was going to make it out, and when she did, she was going to make sure everyone who betrayed her paid in blood.

As the van sped into the night, Jasmine knew one thing for sure: the war wasn't over. Not by a long shot.

And when the dust finally settled, she was going to be the one left standing—no matter who she had to take down to get there.

Chapter 12: Arrest and Betrayal

The night was thick with tension, the kind of tension that makes the hairs on the back of your neck stand up. Jasmine knew something was coming, but the weight of it hit her like a freight train when the blue and red lights flashed in the rearview mirror. The van screeched to a halt as they reached a dead-end alley, the sound of tires skidding on wet pavement echoing through the darkened streets.

"Shit, they got us cornered!" Tasha yelled, her voice trembling with fear and adrenaline.

Jasmine's heart pounded in her chest as she scanned the alleyway, looking for an escape route, but there was none. The Feds had them boxed in tight, like rats in a trap. She could hear the shouts of officers, the clatter of heavy boots hitting the pavement as they moved in.

Marcus sat still in the driver's seat, his hands gripping the steering wheel so tight his knuckles were white. He didn't move, didn't say a word, and that's when Jasmine knew. He'd led them here, straight into the jaws of the beast.

"Marcus, what the fuck did you do?" Jasmine demanded, her voice low and dangerous.

He turned to look at her, and for the first time, Jasmine saw it—saw the truth in his eyes, the cold calculation, the betrayal. "I did what I had to do, Jas," he said, his voice calm, almost resigned. "It was you or me."

Jasmine's stomach twisted with rage and disbelief. "You set me up. You fucking sold me out!"

Marcus didn't flinch, didn't even try to deny it. Instead, a smirk tugged at the corner of his lips, a cruel, twisted satisfaction that made Jasmine's blood boil. "I told you, Jas. You ain't the only one with skin in this game."

Before Jasmine could react, the van's doors were yanked open, and they were dragged out into the cold night air. The Feds were all over them, shouting commands, guns drawn, their faces hard and unyielding. Jasmine's wrists were yanked behind her back, the cold steel of handcuffs biting into her skin as they slammed her against the van.

"Jasmine Washington, you're under arrest for racketeering, drug trafficking, murder, and conspiracy," the lead agent barked, his voice like gravel. "You have the right to remain silent—"

But Jasmine wasn't listening. Her mind was spinning, her vision narrowing as she tried to process what was happening. She'd been betrayed, sold out by the one person she thought she could trust, and now everything she'd built was crumbling around her.

As they shoved her into the back of a squad car, she caught one last glimpse of Marcus, standing off to the side, his face shadowed but that damn smirk still there, mocking her, reveling in his victory.

The ride to the precinct was a blur of flashing lights and blaring sirens. Jasmine sat in the back of the squad car, her mind racing, trying to piece together how everything had fallen apart so quickly. The realization that she'd been played, that Marcus had been working with the Feds all along, gnawed at her, the betrayal cutting deeper than any wound.

She thought about her crew, her empire, the life she'd built brick by brick, only to have it all come crashing down in one devastating blow. And now, as she sat in the cold, hard seat, the reality of her situation sank in. She was done. The queen of the streets had been dethroned, brought low by the very people she'd trusted the most.

The precinct was a hive of activity when they arrived, officers moving with purpose, the air thick with the smell of sweat, coffee, and stale cigarettes. They hauled Jasmine out of the car, the fluorescent lights inside the station casting harsh shadows on her face as they marched her through the booking process.

She kept her head high, refusing to give them the satisfaction of seeing her break. But inside, she was raging, seething with anger and pain. Every time she closed her eyes, she saw Marcus's smirk, heard his voice in her head, mocking her, reminding her of how completely she'd been betrayed.

They processed her quickly, snapping mugshots, taking fingerprints, and then she was thrown into a holding cell, the cold metal bars slamming shut behind her with a finality that sent a chill down her spine. Jasmine sat on the narrow bench, staring at the concrete floor, her thoughts racing.

This was it. The end of the line.

News of Jasmine's arrest spread through the streets like wildfire, and the reaction was immediate, electric. People talked in hushed tones, gathering on corners, in barbershops, in the back rooms of clubs, trying to make sense of it all.

"How the hell did they take her down so quick?" one man asked, shaking his head in disbelief as he leaned against a lamppost.

"Word is, she got sold out by one of her own," another replied, his voice low and full of suspicion. "Somebody been workin' with the Feds, playin' both sides."

"Damn, that's cold. But who coulda done it?"

The rumors flew fast and furious, fingers pointing in every direction, but no one knew the full story. All they knew was that Jasmine, the queen who'd ruled these streets with an iron fist, was now behind bars, and the power vacuum she left in her wake was already starting to tear the community apart.

Some felt a grim satisfaction at her downfall, a twisted sense of justice served. Others were angry, fearful of what would happen now that Jasmine was out of the picture. The streets were a jungle, and without her, they were about to become even more dangerous.

But amid the chaos and confusion, one thing was clear: the streets were never going to be the same.

Meanwhile, Marcus was enjoying the spoils of his betrayal. The Feds had promised him a deal—immunity in exchange for Jasmine and her crew. It was a deal he'd taken without hesitation, trading loyalty for freedom, friendship for survival.

He sat in a plush chair in a small, dimly lit room, the sound of papers shuffling the only noise as the lead agent flipped through the files on his desk. Marcus couldn't help but feel a twisted sense of satisfaction. He'd outplayed them all, outsmarted the woman who'd thought she was untouchable.

"Everything looks in order," the agent said finally, pushing the papers toward Marcus. "Sign these, and you're a free man."

Marcus took the pen, his smirk widening as he signed his name with a flourish. "So, that's it, huh? I'm clear?"

The agent nodded, his expression unreadable. "You're clear. But don't think for a second that you're off the hook. We'll be watching you, Marcus. One wrong move, and you'll be right back where you started."

Marcus shrugged, not particularly worried. He'd played the game and won, and now he was going to reap the rewards. He pushed back his chair, standing up and buttoning his jacket with a practiced ease.

"Pleasure doin' business," he said, his voice dripping with smug satisfaction.

But as he walked out of the room, the door closing behind him with a soft click, a cold wind blew through the corridor, chilling him to the bone. For the first time, Marcus felt a flicker of doubt, a gnawing unease in the pit of his stomach.

He'd won, but at what cost? He'd sold out the only people who'd ever had his back, the only family he'd ever known. And now, as he stepped out into the cold night air, the weight of his betrayal began to settle in.

But it was too late for regrets. Marcus had made his choice, and now he had to live with it—no matter what it cost him.

Back in the cell, Jasmine sat in silence, the cold concrete pressing against her back. The adrenaline had worn off, leaving her with nothing but the hollow ache of betrayal. She thought about her crew, her empire, everything she'd fought so hard to build. And now, it was all gone.

She closed her eyes, taking a deep breath as she tried to steel herself for what was to come. The trial, the sentencing, the years she'd spend behind bars, if she even made it that far. The Feds had her dead to rights, and there was no getting out of this one.

But as she sat there, alone in the darkness, a fire still burned in her chest. They might have taken her freedom, her empire, but they hadn't taken her will to fight. Jasmine wasn't done yet—not by a long shot.

She'd survive this. She'd find a way to rise from the ashes, and when she did, she'd make sure that every single person who betrayed her paid in blood.

Because in the end, there was only one rule on the streets: never back down.

And Jasmine wasn't about to start now.

Chapter 13: Court Appearance

The courtroom was packed, every seat filled, the aisles crowded with people trying to catch a glimpse of Jasmine Washington, the woman who had once ruled the streets. The air was thick with anticipation, the murmurs of the crowd blending into a low hum that buzzed with tension. The media was out in full force, cameras flashing, reporters scribbling notes, eager to capture every moment of what had become the trial of the year.

Jasmine sat at the defense table, her wrists still sore from the cuffs that had bound them just days before. She was dressed in a simple, dark suit, her hair pulled back tight, her face set in a mask of calm defiance. But inside, she was a storm—rage, fear, and betrayal all churning together in a toxic mix.

Her lawyer, a slick-talking defense attorney named Curtis, leaned in close, his voice low. "Jas, they're coming hard. They got evidence, witnesses, everything. But we're gonna fight this. We ain't givin' up."

Jasmine nodded, but her eyes were locked on the prosecutor across the room, a sharp-eyed woman with a reputation for being ruthless. She was sifting through a stack of files, her lips curled in a smug smile that made Jasmine's blood boil. The prosecutor was ready to take her down, and Jasmine knew she had the upper hand. The Feds had built a rock-solid case, and Jasmine was their prize.

The judge entered the courtroom, a stern-faced man who immediately commanded silence. The murmurs died down, replaced by the heavy, expectant quiet that settled over the room like a shroud.

"All rise," the bailiff intoned, and everyone stood as the judge took his seat. "Court is now in session. The United States versus Jasmine Washington."

Jasmine remained standing as the charges were read—racketeering, drug trafficking, conspiracy to commit murder. The words echoed through the courtroom, each one a nail in the coffin of her empire. But she didn't flinch. She wouldn't give them the satisfaction.

The prosecution wasted no time laying out their case, and it was a brutal, relentless assault on everything Jasmine had ever built. They had evidence from the raid, stacks of documents, photos, surveillance footage that painted a damning picture of Jasmine's empire. They brought in witnesses—former associates, rival gang members, even a few of her own crew who had turned against her, trading their loyalty for reduced sentences.

Jasmine watched in silence as one by one, they took the stand, each testimony another blow, another crack in the foundation she had fought so hard to build. The prosecutor, with her cold, calculating gaze, questioned each witness with precision, drawing out every detail, every incriminating piece of evidence.

"Tell the court how you know the defendant," the prosecutor asked one of the witnesses, a man named Mario who had once been one of Jasmine's suppliers.

Mario shifted nervously in his seat, his eyes flicking to Jasmine before he answered. "I—I worked for her. I moved product for her, set up deals, made sure the money kept flowin'."

"And did the defendant ever order you to engage in illegal activities?"

Mario swallowed hard, his voice trembling. "Yeah. She told me what to do, how to do it. If I didn't... well, she made sure I knew the consequences."

The prosecutor nodded, satisfied. "And did you witness the defendant commit any acts of violence in furtherance of her criminal enterprise?"

Mario hesitated, his eyes pleading, but the prosecutor's gaze was unforgiving. "Yes. She... she ordered hits. Had people taken out when they got in her way."

Jasmine clenched her fists under the table, fighting to keep her composure. Mario was lying through his teeth, twisting the truth to save his own skin. But the damage was done. The jury was watching him intently, hanging on every word.

The prosecution continued, methodically dismantling Jasmine's defense, piece by piece. Every witness, every piece of evidence, was another step closer to her downfall. And then, as if the betrayal hadn't cut deep enough, they brought out their star witness—the one person Jasmine had never imagined would turn on her.

Marcus.

When Marcus took the stand, Jasmine felt the air in the courtroom shift, a collective breath being held as everyone waited to see how this would play out. She locked eyes with him, searching for any sign of the man she had once trusted with her life. But all she saw was a stranger—a cold, calculating man who had played her like a pawn.

The prosecutor approached Marcus with a smile that sent a chill down Jasmine's spine. "Mr. Carter, you were once the defendant's closest associate, is that correct?"

Marcus nodded, his expression neutral. "Yeah. We ran things together for years."

"And during that time, did you witness the defendant engage in illegal activities?"

Marcus didn't hesitate. "I did."

The words hung in the air like a death sentence. Jasmine's stomach twisted with a mix of anger and despair. Marcus was really going through with it. He was going to bury her.

"Can you describe some of those activities for the court?" the prosecutor pressed, her voice smooth, almost sympathetic.

Marcus leaned forward slightly, his voice steady. "Jasmine was the mastermind. She ran everything—drugs, money, hits. She made the calls, and everyone followed. If you crossed her, you were done. Simple as that."

Jasmine felt the world tilt, her grip on reality slipping as Marcus's words cut deeper than any knife. She wanted to scream, to deny everything, but she knew it wouldn't matter. Marcus was the final nail in her coffin, and he was hammering it in with a smile.

"Did the defendant ever express any remorse for her actions?" the prosecutor asked, her voice full of feigned curiosity.

Marcus's smirk was almost imperceptible, but Jasmine saw it, and it made her blood run cold. "Remorse? Nah. Jasmine ain't got no remorse. She did what she had to do to keep power. That's all that mattered to her."

Jasmine's lawyer tried to object, but the damage was already done. The jury was staring at Marcus, hanging on his every word. They believed him. Why wouldn't they? He was calm, composed, the perfect witness.

And Jasmine? She was already guilty in their eyes.

As Marcus stepped down from the stand, Jasmine felt the walls of the courtroom closing in on her. The prosecution had played their hand perfectly, and now, as the trial neared its conclusion, Jasmine knew the end was inevitable.

Her lawyer made one last attempt to discredit Marcus, to poke holes in the prosecution's case, but it was clear that the jury had made up their minds. The evidence was overwhelming, the witnesses too credible. And Marcus? He had delivered the killing blow with a precision that left no room for doubt.

The judge called for a recess, and as the courtroom emptied, Jasmine was led back to a holding cell, her mind reeling. She sat on the cold bench, staring at the concrete walls, the reality of her situation sinking in.

She had been betrayed, outplayed, and now, she was facing the consequences. Her empire was gone, her freedom was slipping away, and the streets she had once ruled were buzzing with the news of her downfall.

But as she sat there, a cold resolve settled over her. She wasn't going to go down without a fight. The trial might be nearing its end, but Jasmine wasn't done yet. She had one last card to play, one last move to make.

And when the time came, she was going to make sure that everyone who had crossed her paid the price.

Because in the end, Jasmine Washington wasn't just a victim.

She was a survivor.

And she wasn't going to let them take that away from her.

Chapter 14: Sentencing

The courtroom was packed, just like it had been every day of the trial. But today, the air was different—heavier, more oppressive. The tension was thick, hanging over everyone like a storm about to break. Jasmine sat at the defense table, her hands cuffed in front of her, her face a mask of calm. But beneath that calm, a storm was raging.

She kept her eyes forward, refusing to look at the gallery where the vultures—reporters, curious onlookers, and those who had once feared her—waited to see the final nail driven into her coffin. The judge, an older man with tired eyes, entered the room and took his seat, his expression grim. The gavel came down, the sound echoing through the courtroom like a gunshot.

"This court is now in session for the sentencing of Jasmine Washington," the judge intoned, his voice weary but firm.

Jasmine's lawyer, Curtis, leaned in close, his voice low and urgent. "Jas, whatever happens, keep your head up. Don't let 'em see you break."

Jasmine didn't respond. She didn't need to. She wasn't going to break, not here, not now. She'd survived too much, lost too much to let them see her crumble. But inside, her heart pounded, the weight of everything she'd done, everything she'd lost, pressing down on her like a ton of bricks.

The judge began to speak, his voice a dull drone in Jasmine's ears. He talked about the crimes she'd been convicted of, the lives she'd ruined, the empire she'd built on blood and fear. Jasmine heard the words, but they barely registered. She was too focused on the moment, on the finality of what was about to happen.

"Jasmine Washington," the judge said, his voice cutting through the fog in her mind, "you have been found guilty on all charges. This court sentences you to life in prison without the possibility of parole."

The words hit Jasmine like a sledgehammer, but she didn't flinch. She stared straight ahead, her face expressionless, even as her world came crashing down around her. Life without parole. No way out. No second chances. This was it—the end of the line.

As the judge's words echoed through the courtroom, Jasmine felt the eyes of her crew on her. They were scattered throughout the gallery, the few who had dared to show up, who hadn't already cut ties and run. Tasha was there, her eyes red-rimmed, her face a mask of grief. Malik, her little brother, sat stiffly, his jaw clenched, his hands gripping the edge of the bench so hard his knuckles were white.

Jasmine could feel their pain, their fear, their anger. She'd led them into this war, promised them power, protection, and now, she was leaving them behind to pick up the pieces. The realization twisted like a knife in her gut.

As she was led out of the courtroom, she caught Malik's eye. The look he gave her—full of betrayal, hurt, and a deep, simmering rage—cut deeper than any sentence ever could. She had failed him, failed all of them, and now they were left to fend for themselves in the brutal world she had helped create.

Tasha caught her eye next, her expression one of sorrow and disbelief. They had been through so much together, fought side by side, and now, it was all falling apart. Jasmine wanted to say something, to give her some words of comfort, but nothing came. What could she say? She had led them into the fire, and now they were all burning.

As the guards pulled her away, the courtroom buzzed with whispers, the media already spinning their stories, but Jasmine blocked it all out. All she could think about was the people she had let down, the lives she had destroyed, and the cost of the power she had once craved so desperately.

Back in her cell, the reality of her situation finally began to sink in. The metal door clanged shut behind her, the sound reverberating through the small, sterile space. Jasmine sat down on the narrow cot, her hands still cuffed, her mind racing.

She thought about everything that had led her here—the choices she'd made, the people she'd trusted, the empire she'd built on the backs of those who had followed her. And most of all, she thought about Marcus.

The betrayal still burned in her chest, a constant reminder of how far she had fallen. Marcus had been her right hand, her confidant, the one person she thought she could trust. And in the end, he had been the one to put her in this cage.

Jasmine clenched her fists, the cold metal of the cuffs digging into her skin. She had trusted him, and he had used that trust to destroy everything she had worked for. But as the anger simmered, another thought crept in—a realization that maybe, just maybe, this was the price she had to pay.

The streets had taught her that power came with a cost, and Jasmine had been willing to pay it. But now, sitting alone in this cold, lifeless cell, she wondered if the cost had been too high. She had lost everything—her freedom, her family, her empire—and for what? To be remembered as a queen who had ruled with an iron fist, only to be brought down by her own ambition?

She thought about the people she had hurt, the lives she had taken, the innocent caught in the crossfire of her war. She had justified it all as part of the game, a necessary evil in the pursuit of power. But now, stripped of everything, those justifications felt hollow, empty.

Jasmine closed her eyes, leaning back against the cold wall. There was no going back, no changing what she had done. All she had left was the bitter taste of regret and the knowledge that she had paid the ultimate price for her sins.

Outside the courtroom, the streets were buzzing with the news of Jasmine's sentencing. Word spread fast, faster than any bullet, and the reaction was immediate. Some celebrated, relieved that the queen of the streets had finally been taken down. Others mourned, knowing that with Jasmine gone, the balance of power would shift, and the streets would become even more dangerous.

In the corners of the city, in the alleys and the shadows, people whispered about what would happen next. Without Jasmine, the empire she had built was crumbling, and everyone knew it was only a matter of time before someone else tried to take her place.

But there was also a sense of unease, a feeling that something had been lost. Jasmine had been ruthless, yes, but she had also been a protector, someone who had kept the worst of the chaos at bay. Now, with her gone, the future was uncertain, and the streets were on the brink of exploding into violence.

Malik walked through the neighborhood, the weight of his sister's downfall heavy on his shoulders. He had idolized her, followed in her footsteps, but now he was left with nothing but anger and confusion. The streets were talking, and he could feel the eyes on him, the expectations, the fear. People wondered what he would do, if he would try to fill the void Jasmine had left behind.

But Malik didn't know. All he knew was that the world felt colder, darker, without his sister in it.

Back in her cell, Jasmine stared at the ceiling, her mind drifting over the past, the choices she had made, the people she had loved and lost. The pain of betrayal still lingered, but now it was joined by something else—a deep, gnawing emptiness that threatened to swallow her whole.

She had been a queen, but now she was nothing more than a number, a name on a docket, a prisoner locked away for the rest of her life. The power she had once wielded was gone, the empire she had built reduced to rubble.

But even in the darkness, Jasmine felt a flicker of defiance. They had taken everything from her, but they hadn't broken her. She was still Jasmine Washington, still the woman who had fought her way to the top, and she wasn't going to let them see her crumble.

The streets had made her, and they had unmade her. But deep down, she knew that she was more than just a product of the life she had lived. She was a survivor, and even in this cold, empty cell, she would find a way to keep fighting.

Because that's what she did.

She survived.

And no one, not Marcus, not the Feds, not the judge, could take that away from her.

Chapter 15: The Fall of the Empire

The morning was cold, the sky gray and unforgiving, as the Feds moved in like a swarm of locusts. They hit every spot at once—Jasmine's safehouses, her stash spots, the fronts she'd used to wash her money clean. Nothing was spared. Her empire, built on blood, sweat, and ruthless ambition, was being torn apart piece by piece, brick by brick.

Agents in dark suits and tactical gear stormed through the streets, shoving aside anyone who got in their way. They kicked in doors, dragged out Jasmine's people, and loaded them into waiting vans. Her crew, the ones who hadn't already scattered to the wind, were rounded up, cuffed, and tossed aside like garbage.

Jasmine's assets were seized with cold efficiency. The cars, the cash, the properties—all of it was gone in a flash, wiped off the board as if it had never existed. The people who had once feared and respected her watched from the shadows, whispering among themselves, trying to make sense of the chaos.

"This shit's wild," a young hustler muttered, leaning against a streetlamp as he watched the Feds load up a convoy of luxury cars. "Jas had all this locked down, and now... look at it. Gone, just like that."

"Yeah, but you know how it is," another replied, his voice low and wary. "Ain't nobody safe in this game. They take you out as fast as they put you on top."

The streets buzzed with the news, word spreading like wildfire. Jasmine's empire was crumbling, and everyone knew it. The power she had wielded so effortlessly was slipping through her fingers, and the streets were left reeling from the sudden shift.

With Jasmine's empire in ruins, the streets were thrown into disarray. The power vacuum left by her downfall created a dangerous void, one that the wolves of the city were all too eager to fill. Rival crews began to circle like vultures, each one looking to snatch up a piece of what had once been Jasmine's territory.

The corners that had been under Jasmine's control were now battlegrounds, the sound of gunfire echoing through the alleys as old scores were settled and new beefs were born. The fragile alliances Jasmine had maintained fell apart, replaced by violence and betrayal as everyone scrambled to claim a piece of the crumbling empire.

In the absence of a strong hand to keep order, the streets descended into chaos. The rules that had once kept things in check were gone, replaced by the law of the jungle, where only the strongest survived.

Tasha, one of the few remaining loyal to Jasmine, found herself caught in the middle of the madness. She had managed to avoid the Feds' sweep, but now she was left with nothing—no protection, no crew, no leader. The streets she had once ruled with Jasmine were now a war zone, and she was just another target.

"Fuck, this shit's gone to hell," Tasha muttered under her breath as she ducked into a corner store, trying to catch her breath. She knew she couldn't stay out in the open for long. Too many people would be gunning for her now, trying to take advantage of the power shift.

The store's owner, an old man who had seen more than his fair share of street wars, shook his head as he watched Tasha. "Girl, you better get outta here before they catch you. Ain't no safety out there no more. Not with Jas gone."

Tasha nodded, her mind racing as she tried to figure out her next move. Jasmine had been her anchor, the one who had kept everything together. But now, with Jasmine behind bars and the empire in ruins, Tasha was adrift, left to navigate the dangerous waters of the streets on her own.

As the streets erupted in violence, the community that had once thrived under Jasmine's rule began to suffer. Without her iron fist to keep the worst elements in check, the neighborhood fell into chaos. Businesses that had paid Jasmine for protection were now at the mercy of thugs and extortionists. The people who had once relied on Jasmine to keep the peace found themselves caught in the crossfire.

Malik, Jasmine's younger brother, walked through the neighborhood, his heart heavy with anger and despair. He had looked up to his sister, had seen her as a protector, someone who had fought for their family and their community. But now, all of that was gone, and the world he had known was crumbling around him.

He passed by the bodega where he used to buy candy as a kid, now a boarded-up wreck after a shootout had left the place riddled with bullets. The old man who ran the place was gone, replaced by a gang of young thugs who leaned against the walls, their eyes hard and unforgiving.

"Yo, Malik," one of them called out, a sneer on his face. "Heard your sister got locked up. Guess that means you on your own now, huh?"

Malik clenched his fists, his jaw tight. He knew better than to respond, knew that any sign of weakness would be exploited. But the anger burned in his chest, a fire that wouldn't be quenched.

He kept walking, his mind racing as he thought about everything that had happened. Jasmine had been their protector, but now she was gone, and the neighborhood was paying the price. The people who had once feared her now feared for their lives, and the streets were soaked in blood.

Malik knew he had to do something, but what? He was just one person, a kid who had lost everything. The empire his sister had built was gone, and all that was left was the ruins, the ashes of a dream that had turned into a nightmare.

As the days passed, the struggle for control of Jasmine's former empire intensified. The gangs that had once been held in check by her power now fought tooth and nail to claim what was left. The city was a battlefield, and the casualties mounted as each faction tried to assert its dominance.

Tasha, still on the run, tried to rally the few remaining loyalists, but it was a losing battle. The power structure that Jasmine had carefully constructed had collapsed, and there was no one left to pick up the pieces. The alliances that had once been the backbone of her empire were shattered, replaced by a brutal free-for-all that threatened to tear the city apart.

She met with a few of the old crew in a dingy basement, the air thick with tension and the smell of sweat. "We gotta do somethin', Tash," one of the men said, his voice low and desperate. "We can't just let this shit fall apart."

Tasha shook her head, frustration and fear warring inside her. "What the fuck you think we can do? Jas is gone, and they takin' everything we had. We ain't got no muscle, no money. Nothin'."

"But we can't just sit back and watch, either," another man argued, his eyes wild with desperation. "They're gonna come for us next. We gotta strike first, take back what's ours."

Tasha looked around the room, saw the fear and uncertainty in their faces, and knew that it was over. Jasmine's empire was dead, and there was no bringing it back. The streets had moved on, and the new order was being established in blood and fire.

"We gotta lay low," Tasha finally said, her voice heavy with resignation. "Ain't no winnin' this fight. Not now. We gotta survive, and then... we see what's left."

The fall of Jasmine's empire sent shockwaves through the city, leaving a trail of destruction and despair in its wake. The power vacuum she left behind was filled with violence, as rival factions tore each other apart in a bid for control. The streets that had once been under her command were now battlegrounds, the city gripped by fear and uncertainty.

But amid the chaos, there was a sense of finality, a realization that the world had changed, and there was no going back. Jasmine's empire had fallen, and with it, the fragile order she had maintained. The streets were in disarray, the community reeling from the sudden shift in power.

As Malik walked through the wreckage of his sister's dream, he felt a deep, simmering rage in his chest. The world he had known was gone, destroyed by the very forces that had once held it together. But in the ruins, he also saw a glimmer of something else—a chance to rebuild, to create something new out of the ashes.

But that would come later. For now, all Malik could do was survive.

The city was in ruins, and the empire that Jasmine had built was gone.

But the streets would never forget her name.

And neither would Malik.

Chapter 16: Alone in the Cell

The heavy clank of the metal door echoed in Jasmine's ears, the sound sealing her fate as it shut behind her. She stood in the middle of the tiny cell, her new world reduced to four cold, concrete walls and a narrow cot. The air was thick with the stench of despair, sweat, and fear, the same scent that clung to the walls of every prison she'd ever heard of. But now, this wasn't just a story from the streets. It was her reality.

Jasmine took a deep breath, trying to push down the rising panic that threatened to choke her. She couldn't let herself break. Not now. Not after everything. She'd been the queen of the streets, had ruled with an iron fist, and now... now she was just another inmate, stripped of her power, her freedom, her name.

She sat down on the cot, the thin mattress offering no comfort, and stared at the gray walls, her mind racing. The sound of distant screams and the clatter of metal echoed through the halls, a constant reminder of where she was, what she had lost. But even as the darkness closed in around her, Jasmine refused to give in. She couldn't afford to. There was still too much to do, too much unfinished business.

"Marcus," she whispered, the name a curse on her lips. The thought of him, the man who had betrayed her, who had sold her out, filled her with a cold, burning rage. She could still see his smirk, the satisfaction in his eyes as he testified against her, as he twisted the knife he'd stabbed into her back.

Jasmine clenched her fists, her nails digging into her palms until she felt the sting of pain. She welcomed it, embraced it, let it fuel the fire inside her. She'd survive this. She had to. And when the time came, she'd make sure Marcus paid for what he'd done.

The days in the high-security prison bled into each other, a monotonous routine of harsh lights, cold showers, and the constant threat of violence. Jasmine quickly learned that the world behind bars was a different kind of jungle, where power was measured not by money or territory, but by fear and respect.

She kept to herself at first, watching, listening, learning the unspoken rules that governed life inside. The other inmates eyed her with a mix of curiosity and suspicion, trying to figure out where she fit in the hierarchy. Jasmine could see the predators, the ones who thrived on the chaos, who would test her if they saw any sign of weakness.

She wasn't about to give them that satisfaction.

Her first encounter came in the yard, during the mandatory exercise period. Jasmine was doing push-ups, trying to burn off the restless energy that had been building inside her since the moment she stepped through the prison gates, when a group of women approached. They were hard, their faces marked with the scars of countless battles, their eyes cold and calculating.

"What you think you doin' here, bitch?" the leader, a tall woman with a shaved head and a tattoo of a spider on her neck, sneered. "This ain't the streets. You ain't queen here."

Jasmine didn't stop, didn't even look up. "I ain't lookin' to be no queen," she said evenly, her voice calm but edged with steel. "I'm just doin' my time."

The woman laughed, a harsh, grating sound. "Time? Bitch, you ain't gonna last a week if you don't show some respect."

Jasmine finally stood up, wiping the sweat from her brow as she looked the woman dead in the eye. "Respect? I don't know you, and I don't give a fuck 'bout your respect. You got a problem with that, then do somethin'."

The challenge hung in the air, the tension thick enough to cut with a knife. The other inmates in the yard went silent, watching, waiting to see what would happen. The woman's eyes narrowed, her muscles tensing as she weighed her options.

But Jasmine didn't flinch, didn't back down. She knew how this game worked. Show fear, show weakness, and you were done. But if you stood your ground, if you proved you weren't afraid, they'd think twice before coming at you.

After what felt like an eternity, the woman smirked, a glint of grudging respect in her eyes. "Aight, then. We'll see how long you last."

She turned and walked away, her crew following her, but Jasmine knew it wasn't over. It was never over. Not in here. She'd made it through the first test, but there would be others. And she had to be ready.

The worst part of prison wasn't the violence, the constant threat of attack, or even the suffocating routine. It was the isolation. The feeling of being cut off from the outside world, from everything and everyone she'd ever known. Jasmine had always been surrounded by people, by noise, by life. But now, in the cold, dark cell, she was alone.

Days turned into weeks, weeks into months, and the reality of her situation settled over her like a thick, suffocating blanket. There was no escape, no way out. The life she had lived, the power she had wielded, was gone, reduced to nothing but memories.

But even in the darkest moments, when the weight of it all threatened to crush her, Jasmine held onto one thought, one burning desire that kept her going: revenge. She'd make Marcus pay. She didn't know how, or when, but she would. And that thought, that promise, was the only thing that kept her from giving in to the despair that lurked in the corners of her mind.

Jasmine spent hours lying on her cot, staring at the ceiling, her mind racing with plans, schemes, possibilities. She couldn't do anything from inside these walls, but that didn't mean she couldn't plan. She had people on the outside, people who were still loyal, still owed her. And when the time was right, she'd call in those favors.

But for now, she had to survive. She had to play the game, bide her time, and wait for her moment.

As the weeks went by, Jasmine began to navigate the complex web of prison politics. She knew how to read people, how to gauge who was worth aligning with and who was better left alone. It was a skill she had honed on the streets, and it served her well in here.

She started making connections, carefully choosing who to associate with and who to avoid. There were the lifers, the ones who had accepted their fate and carved out their own little kingdoms inside the walls. Then there were the short-timers, the ones just trying to keep their heads down and get through their sentences. And then there were the predators, the ones who thrived on the violence, who saw every day as a chance to climb higher in the twisted hierarchy.

Jasmine walked a fine line, balancing between showing strength and not drawing too much attention to herself. She didn't want to become a target, but she also couldn't afford to be seen as weak. She made a few allies, people who had their own reasons for sticking close to her, but she kept them at arm's length. Trust was a luxury she couldn't afford anymore.

One day, she was approached by a woman named Rosa, a tough, battle-hardened inmate who had been running things in her block for years. Rosa had heard about Jasmine, about her past, and was curious.

"You got a rep, girl," Rosa said, leaning against the wall of the yard as they watched the other inmates milling around. "Word is, you used to run shit on the outside."

Jasmine shrugged, not giving anything away. "Used to. Now I'm just tryin' to survive, same as everyone else."

Rosa nodded, her eyes sharp and calculating. "Survival's the name of the game in here. But you ain't like the rest of these bitches. You got fire. I can see it."

Jasmine didn't respond, just kept her eyes on the yard, watching the ebb and flow of power among the inmates. Rosa was right, of course. She still had that fire, that drive, but it was different now. More focused, more dangerous.

"You ever need somethin', you come to me," Rosa continued, her voice low. "I got connections, ways to make things happen. Just remember—ain't nothin' free in here."

Jasmine nodded, filing the information away. She knew better than to trust Rosa, but alliances were necessary in a place like this. She'd play the game, make the deals, but she'd never forget why she was really here.

As the days turned into months, Jasmine's resolve only grew stronger. The anger, the betrayal, the loss—they all fueled her, pushed her to keep going. She refused to let this be the end. She had survived the streets, survived the war, and she'd survive this, too.

But she knew she couldn't do it alone. She needed to find a way to reach out, to connect with the people who were still loyal to her on the outside. She started making plans, carefully piecing together a network that could help her when the time was right.

She used every resource she had, every connection she could find, to start laying the groundwork for her eventual revenge. It wouldn't be easy, and it wouldn't happen overnight, but Jasmine was patient. She had nothing but time, and she'd use it to her advantage.

She began sending messages through the few trusted inmates she had befriended, passing along coded notes that would make their way to the outside. Slowly but surely, she began to rebuild her network, one piece at a time.

Every night, as she lay in her cell, Jasmine thought about Marcus, about how he had betrayed her, and about how she would make him pay. The thought of revenge kept her warm, kept her sane, even as the cold reality of prison life tried to break her down.

But Jasmine Washington wasn't broken. Not yet.

She was a survivor, and she'd survive this, too.

And when the time came, she'd remind everyone who she really was.

The queen might be in a cage, but she was still a queen.

And she'd make damn sure Marcus—and everyone else—never forgot that.

Chapter 17: Marcus's Reign

Marcus leaned back in the plush leather chair, his fingers wrapped around a crystal glass of top-shelf whiskey. The office he now occupied was a far cry from the cramped, dingy rooms where he and Jasmine used to plan their moves. This place, with its polished wood and floor-to-ceiling windows overlooking the city, was a testament to his new position of power. He was no longer the man in the shadows, playing second fiddle to a queen. Now, he was the one calling the shots.

The night air was thick with the scent of rain, the streets below glistening under the neon lights of the city. Marcus took a slow sip of his drink, savoring the burn as it slid down his throat. This was what he had always wanted—control, power, the respect that came with being the man on top. And now, with Jasmine locked away, there was nothing standing in his way.

A knock at the door pulled him from his thoughts. He didn't bother to look up as one of his new lieutenants stepped in, a skinny kid with nervous eyes who was eager to prove himself. Marcus didn't remember his name, didn't care to.

"Everything's set, boss," the kid said, his voice shaky. "The shipment's coming in tomorrow night. We got the muscle in place, too. Ain't nobody gonna fuck with us."

Marcus nodded, his gaze still fixed on the city outside. "Good. Make sure it goes smooth. I don't want no fuck-ups. We gotta show these streets who's in charge now."

The kid nodded quickly, eager to please. "Yeah, boss. No fuck-ups. I'll make sure of it."

As the kid left, Marcus allowed himself a small smile. The power he held now was intoxicating, a drug that fueled his every move. But it wasn't just about the money or the control—it was about respect. The kind of respect Jasmine had always had, but Marcus had never truly tasted until now. And it was sweet.

But with power came enemies, and Marcus knew that the throne he now sat on was a precarious one. The streets were buzzing with the news of Jasmine's downfall, and while many were ready to bow down to the new king, there were others who saw an opportunity to take what was his.

The streets were alive with gossip, every corner buzzing with the latest word on Marcus's rise to power. Some respected him, others feared him, but everyone was talking about him. The fall of Jasmine had left a vacuum, and Marcus had wasted no time in filling it. But the way he had done it—betrayal, manipulation, selling out his own crew—left a sour taste in the mouths of many.

In the back room of a rundown bar, a group of street hustlers huddled around a table, their voices low but intense.

"Man, you hear what Marcus did to Jasmine? That shit's cold, bro," one of them muttered, shaking his head in disbelief.

"Yeah, but he got the juice now," another replied, his tone tinged with both awe and fear. "Ain't nobody gonna step to him. He got the Feds on his side, too. You cross him, you end up like Jas."

"Still, though," the first man said, his voice dropping to a whisper. "You can't trust a nigga who'd do that to his own people. What's to say he won't do the same to you?"

The others nodded in agreement, their eyes darting around the room as if Marcus himself might be lurking in the shadows, listening to their every word. The truth was, Marcus had become a figure of both fear and loathing, a man who had betrayed his way to the top and now sat on a throne built on the ruins of Jasmine's empire.

But fear could only carry a man so far. Respect had to be earned, and Marcus knew that. He had seen what happened to those who ruled through fear alone—they fell, and they fell hard. Jasmine had taught him that lesson, even if she hadn't meant to.

Marcus wasted no time in consolidating his power. He knew that the streets were watching, waiting to see if he would stumble, if he could hold on to the empire he had taken. He moved quickly, taking control of Jasmine's old territories, making deals with those who had been loyal to her but were now looking for a new leader.

He kept his operations tight, using the connections he had built with the Feds to keep his enemies in check. Anyone who posed a threat, anyone who even thought about challenging him, was quickly dealt with. Marcus had learned from the best—Jasmine had been ruthless, and now he was, too.

But Marcus was also smart. He knew that brute force alone wouldn't be enough to keep him on top. He needed allies, people who would stand by him not out of fear, but out of loyalty. He started making moves, reaching out to the smaller crews, the independent hustlers who had been pushed to the margins by Jasmine's reign.

He offered them protection, a piece of the action, a seat at the table. And in return, they gave him their loyalty. Marcus was building a new kind of empire, one that wasn't just held together by fear, but by mutual interest. He knew that this was the only way to ensure his rule would last.

As Marcus solidified his power on the streets, he also began to cultivate a public image. He wasn't just a kingpin, he was a man of the people—or at least, that's what he wanted everyone to believe. He started making appearances in the community, donating money to local schools, funding food drives, and making sure his name was associated with good deeds as well as criminal activity.

The media picked up on it, and soon, Marcus was being painted as a complex figure—a man who had come from nothing, who had clawed his way to the top, but who hadn't forgotten where he came from. Some called him a savior, a man who was trying to give back to the community he had once terrorized. Others saw through the facade, recognizing it for what it was—a calculated move to solidify his power and protect his empire.

But it didn't matter what people thought. What mattered was that Marcus was creating a narrative, one that would make it harder for his enemies to take him down. He wasn't just a criminal, he was a figure of influence, a man who could sway public opinion in his favor.

And for a while, it worked. The streets began to quiet down, the violence that had erupted after Jasmine's fall started to subside as Marcus tightened his grip on the city. People began to accept his rule, to see him as the new king of the streets.

But Marcus knew better than to get comfortable. The throne he sat on was a fragile one, and there were always those who would want to knock him off it.

With power came consequences, and Marcus was no stranger to that fact. The more control he gained, the more enemies he made. The whispers on the streets, the murmurs of dissent—they never fully went away. And Marcus, for all his intelligence and ruthlessness, couldn't shake the feeling that his empire was built on shaky ground.

The first real challenge to his reign came from an unexpected quarter—a group of old-school hustlers who had been loyal to Jasmine and were not happy with the way Marcus had taken her down. They saw him as a traitor, a man who had sold out his own people for power, and they weren't about to let him rule without a fight.

The attack came one night as Marcus was leaving one of his clubs, a high-end spot that had become the center of his new empire. He was flanked by his bodyguards, but they were caught off guard when the shots rang out, echoing through the narrow streets.

Marcus hit the ground, rolling behind a car as bullets whizzed past his head. His men returned fire, and for a few minutes, the street was a war zone, the sound of gunfire and screams filling the night air.

When it was over, Marcus emerged from behind the car, shaken but unharmed. His bodyguards had taken down the attackers, leaving their bodies sprawled on the pavement, but the message was clear—Marcus's rule was not as secure as he thought.

The attack rattled him, but it also steeled his resolve. He couldn't afford to show weakness, couldn't afford to let anyone see that he was anything less than in control. He doubled down on his efforts, tightening his grip on the city, making sure that anyone who dared to challenge him would regret it.

The streets were alive with the news of the attack, and the reaction was mixed. Some saw it as a sign that Marcus was vulnerable, that his enemies were growing bolder. Others saw it as proof that Marcus was the real deal, a man who could take a hit and keep going.

But one thing was clear—the streets were watching, waiting to see what would happen next. Marcus's reign was still new, still untested, and there were plenty of people who wanted to see him fall.

In the backrooms of clubs, in the shadows of alleyways, people talked about the man who had betrayed Jasmine and taken her throne. Some respected him, some feared him, but no one trusted him. Marcus had made his bed, and now he had to lie in it.

But Marcus wasn't worried. He had come too far, sacrificed too much, to let anyone take what was his.

Chapter 18: Lingering Tensions

The city was a ticking time bomb, and everyone knew it. With Jasmine behind bars, the fragile order she had maintained was shattered. Her former allies and the remnants of the Black Knights were locked in a brutal struggle for power, each one trying to carve out their own piece of the empire she had left behind. The streets were stained with blood, every corner buzzing with tension as old grudges flared into open warfare.

Tasha had managed to keep her head down, but she could feel the heat rising all around her. The once-powerful alliances that Jasmine had forged were crumbling, and the void left by her absence had turned the streets into a battleground. Crews that had once worked together now fought for dominance, and the Black Knights—those who had survived Jasmine's wrath—were making a comeback, hungry for revenge and eager to reclaim what they had lost.

"Shit's wild out here," Tasha muttered, leaning against the wall of a grimy alley as she lit a cigarette. Her eyes darted around, ever watchful for any sign of trouble. She had heard about the latest hit—two of Jasmine's old lieutenants gunned down in broad daylight, their bodies left as a message for anyone still loyal to her.

"Yeah, but it ain't just us," said Slim, a skinny, jittery kid who had once run errands for Jasmine. "The Black Knights, they're comin' hard. They want their territory back, and they ain't playin'. We gotta watch our backs."

Tasha took a drag from her cigarette, her mind racing. She had known this was coming—the minute Jasmine went down, the streets were gonna eat each other alive. But she wasn't ready to give up just yet. "We need to move smart, Slim. Ain't no loyalty left in these streets, but we gotta survive. Keep your head low, stay outta the crossfire."

Slim nodded, his eyes wide with fear. "But what 'bout Marcus? He's the one sittin' on the throne now. Ain't he gonna do somethin'?"

Tasha scoffed, shaking her head. "Marcus? That nigga's too busy tryna play king to care 'bout what's happenin' down here. He thinks he's untouchable, but he's gonna learn real quick that these streets don't forget. Jasmine might be locked up, but her shadow's still castin' long."

As they talked, the sound of sirens wailed in the distance, a constant reminder that the city was on the brink. The power struggle was far from over, and with every day that passed, the tension only grew.

The battle for control wasn't just about territory—it was about survival. The old alliances that had once held the streets together were dissolving, replaced by new ones formed out of necessity and desperation. Trust was a currency that had lost all its value, and betrayal was the language everyone spoke.

In the dimly lit back room of a rundown bar, a group of former Black Knights sat around a table, their faces hard and unforgiving. They had lost everything when Jasmine took them down, and now they were out for blood, ready to reclaim what was theirs.

"Jasmine's gone, but her people are still out there," said Cruz, a grizzled veteran of the streets who had once been a top enforcer for the Black Knights. "We gotta hit 'em hard, take back what's ours before Marcus gets his claws in any deeper."

"Marcus is a snake," another man growled, his fists clenched on the table. "But he's got the Feds on his side. We go up against him, we gotta be ready for the heat."

Cruz nodded, his eyes narrowing. "That's why we need allies. There's plenty of folks out there who ain't happy with the way things went down. We find 'em, bring 'em to our side, and we take Marcus down, piece by piece."

The plan was risky, but they were desperate. The Black Knights had been a force to be reckoned with, and they weren't about to let their legacy be erased by a man like Marcus. But the streets were different now—more volatile, more unpredictable. And Cruz knew that if they wanted to survive, they had to adapt.

Meanwhile, on the other side of town, those who had once been loyal to Jasmine were having their own conversations, plotting their next moves. They knew that they were targets, that Marcus was watching them, waiting for any sign of rebellion. But they also knew that the power he held was built on shaky ground, and all it would take was one good push to bring it all crashing down.

But no matter where the alliances shifted, one thing remained constant: the name Jasmine Washington still carried weight, still inspired both fear and respect. And that was something Marcus could never erase.

In the darkness of her cell, Jasmine lay on the thin mattress, her eyes closed, her mind a storm of thoughts. The isolation, the monotony, the crushing weight of her new reality—it all pressed down on her, threatening to suffocate her. But even in the deepest moments of despair, she refused to let go of her anger, her thirst for revenge.

Sleep came in fits and starts, haunted by memories of the life she had lost, the empire she had built, and the betrayal that had brought it all crashing down. And then, one night, as she drifted off into a restless sleep, she found herself standing in a place she hadn't seen in months—the old warehouse where she and Marcus used to meet, where they had planned and plotted their rise to power.

But something was different. The air was thick with tension, the shadows longer and darker than she remembered. And there, in the center of the room, stood Marcus, his back to her, his hands clasped behind him.

Jasmine's heart pounded in her chest as she took a step forward, her fists clenched at her sides. "Marcus," she said, her voice low and dangerous.

He turned to face her, his expression unreadable, but there was something in his eyes—a flicker of fear, perhaps, or maybe guilt. "Jas," he said, his voice smooth but hollow. "I didn't expect to see you here."

Jasmine felt the rage bubbling up inside her, the fire that had been burning ever since the moment he betrayed her. "You think this is over, Marcus? You think you can just take what's mine and walk away clean?"

Marcus smirked, but it didn't reach his eyes. "It's already over, Jas. You lost. You're in a cell, and I'm out here, running things. You can't touch me."

Jasmine took another step forward, her eyes locked on his. "You think I can't reach you from in here? You think you're safe? You're a fool, Marcus. I might be locked up, but I still got people out there. And they know what you did."

Marcus's smirk faltered, just for a second, and Jasmine saw it—the crack in his armor, the doubt that had been gnawing at him ever since he took her down. "You're bluffing," he said, but his voice lacked its usual confidence.

"You know I ain't bluffin'," Jasmine shot back. "You're gonna pay for what you did, Marcus. Maybe not today, maybe not tomorrow, but I'm gonna make sure you pay. And when I'm done, you're gonna wish you never crossed me."

The warehouse seemed to close in around them, the air thick with unspoken words, with the weight of their history, their betrayal. Jasmine could see the fear in Marcus's eyes now, the realization that he wasn't as untouchable as he thought.

"Enjoy your throne while you can," Jasmine said, her voice a low growl. "Because it won't be long before it crumbles beneath you."

And with that, she turned and walked away, the darkness swallowing her up as the warehouse faded from view. But even as she left, she could feel Marcus's eyes on her, the fear and uncertainty she had planted in his mind taking root.

Back in her cell, Jasmine woke with a start, the dream still fresh in her mind. The confrontation with Marcus had felt so real, so vivid, and she knew that it wasn't just a figment of her imagination. It was a reminder, a message to herself that she wasn't done yet.

She sat up, the cold air of the cell biting at her skin, and let her thoughts settle. Marcus might have taken her empire, might have betrayed her in the worst way possible, but she was still Jasmine Washington. And as long as she was alive, her legacy would live on.

Jasmine had always been a fighter, a survivor, and this was just another battle. She might be behind bars, but her influence still reached far beyond the prison walls. She knew that the streets were still talking about her, that her name still carried weight. And she would use that to her advantage.

Over the next few days, Jasmine began to plan, to reach out to the few contacts she still had. It wasn't easy—communication in prison was limited, monitored, and she had to be careful. But she was patient, methodical, and slowly but surely, she started to rebuild her network.

She knew she couldn't take Marcus down from behind bars, but she didn't need to. All she had to do was plant the seeds, set things in motion, and let the streets do the rest. Marcus might be sitting on the throne now, but Jasmine was going to make sure that throne turned to dust beneath him.

And as she sat in her cell, the cold concrete walls closing in around her, Jasmine felt something she hadn't felt in a long time—hope. Not the kind of hope that comes from wishing for something better, but the kind that comes from knowing you still have the power to change your fate.

Jasmine leaned back against the wall, her eyes closed, a small smile playing on her lips. She could feel the fire burning inside her, the determination that had always driven her, and she knew that she wasn't done yet.

The cell might be her prison, but it was also her sanctuary, a place where she could focus, plan, and prepare. She was confined, but she wasn't defeated. Not by a long shot.

The streets were still in chaos, the power struggle far from over, and Jasmine knew that her legacy would continue to shape the city, even from behind bars. She had built something that couldn't be destroyed by one man's betrayal, something that would live on long after she was gone.

And as long as she had that, as long as she had her resolve, Jasmine knew that she could survive anything.

Marcus might be the king for now, but he was sitting on borrowed time. Jasmine had lost the battle, but the war was far from over. And when the time came, she would make sure Marcus felt the full weight of her wrath.

Because Jasmine Washington wasn't just a name. It was a legacy, a force to be reckoned with.

And no one—not Marcus, not the Feds, not the walls of this prison—could take that away from her.

The queen might be locked up, but she was far from finished. And she always came back from anything!

Don't miss out!

Visit the website below and you can sign up to receive emails whenever Rachael Reed publishes a new book. There's no charge and no obligation.

https://books2read.com/r/B-A-WXARB-ANPUE

BOOKS 2 READ

Connecting independent readers to independent writers.

Did you love *Sis 2 Blood on the Streets*? Then you should read *SIS*[1] by Rachael Reed!

[2]

Sis: A Tale of Power and Betrayal

In the heart of Richmond's unforgiving streets, Jasmine has clawed her way to the top, ruling her empire with an iron fist and a sharp mind. Born into the harsh realities of the ghetto, she turned to the drug game to escape poverty, becoming a formidable force in a world dominated by betrayal, violence, and survival. But power comes at a price, and the streets are always hungry for blood.

Jasmine's journey is one of relentless ambition and ruthless determination. From small-time hustling to partnering with the notorious Dre, she learned the rules of the game the hard way. When Dre's betrayal threatened everything she had built, Jasmine took

---

1. https://books2read.com/u/mZlxoR

2. https://books2read.com/u/mZlxoR

matters into her own hands, proving that she's not one to be crossed. Now, as the queen of Richmond's underworld, she faces new enemies and internal power struggles that could bring her empire crashing down.

As Jasmine fights to maintain her reign, she grapples with the personal cost of her decisions. Guilt, regret, and the loss of innocence weigh heavily on her, even as she seeks redemption by giving back to her community. But the streets are relentless, and new threats emerge, testing her strategic brilliance and unyielding resolve.

In a world where trust is a luxury and betrayal lurks around every corner, Jasmine must navigate the treacherous waters of the drug game with cunning and ferocity. The final showdown with a new rival threatens to dismantle everything she has fought for, leading to an explosive climax that will decide the future of her reign.

Sis is a gripping tale of power, survival, and the brutal realities of urban life. With its gritty dialogue, dark undertones, and relentless pace, this novel plunges you into the heart of the streets, where every decision can mean the difference between life and death. Jasmine's story is one of fierce loyalty, calculated moves, and the constant struggle to stay on top in a world that never truly lets go.

Also by Rachael Reed

Sis
Sis 2 Blood on the Streets

Standalone
Codefendant
Codefendant
Once a Cheater
Once a Cheater
Passport Bro
What Happens in Prison
Preference
Sprinkle Sprinkle
Championship Bad
Street Exodus
Street Exodus
Street Royalty
Pawns of Power
SIS
Cartel Bloodline
Get Money Girls
Skip the Games
Til Death Do Us Part

Backpage Hustle
Link in Bio
The Virgin and The Kingpin
A Gangsta's Heart
Boosters
Can't Turn a Hoe Into a Housewife

9 798227 902214